Be kind and compassionate to one another, forgiving
each other, just as in Christ God forgave you.

—Ephesians 4:32 (NIV)

MYSTERIES OF COBBLE HILL FARM

MYSTERIES OF COBBLE HILL FARM

A Little Bird Told Me

LAURA BRADFORD

Guideposts

Mysteries of Cobble Hill Farm is a trademark of Guideposts.

Published by Guideposts
100 Reserve Road, Suite E200, Danbury, CT 06810
Guideposts.org

Cover and interior design by Müllerhaus
Cover illustration by Bob Kayganich at Illustration Online LLC.
Typeset by Aptara, Inc.

ISBN 978-1-961251-68-7 (hardcover)
ISBN 978-1-961251-69-4 (softcover)
ISBN 978-1-961251-70-0 (epub)

Printed and bound in the United States of America

MYSTERIES OF COBBLE HILL FARM

A Little Bird Told Me

GLOSSARY OF UK TERMS

bloke • man

brolly • umbrella

car park • parking lot

chuffed • pleased, delighted

daft • crazy

loo • bathroom

pram • baby carriage or stroller

CHAPTER ONE

Sinking down onto the edge of the closest waiting room chair, Harriet Bailey released a long sigh of relief. "As good as today was, I'll be mighty glad to shut off the lights the moment you head out to your car."

"I'll be rather chuffed, myself." Polly Thatcher tossed her phone into her tote bag, tugged its strap up her arm, and pushed her desk drawer shut. "But today really was fantastic, wasn't it? A new patient, two boarders scheduled for next week, a successful surgery, and you don't have a single new scratch on you anywhere."

Harriet's answering laugh trailed away as a familiar squeaking sound drew near. A long-haired dachshund scurried into view, thanks to the wheeled prosthesis that had given him a new lease on life. "Tonight's the night, Maxwell. You, me, and a can of oil."

"Must you?" Polly asked, resting her hand on the doorknob. "I've grown rather fond of his squeaking."

Harriet reached down, ran her hand along the dog's back, and then returned it to the top of his head for a much-appreciated scratch behind the ears. "I must. Right, Maxwell?"

At Maxwell's answering lick of her hand, she looked up at her receptionist and best friend in the open doorway. "I imagine your plans for this evening are a bit more exciting than mine."

"That remains to be seen."

"But you have a date with a certain bloke we both know, correct?"

Polly's laugh filled the veterinary reception area. "Look at you, using the word *bloke*. Correctly, even."

"And it sounded natural, right?"

Polly pursed her lips as if weighing Harriet's question. "You're getting there."

"I'll take that." Harriet stood and stretched her back. "Give me another six months, and no one will have any inkling I'm not from White Church Bay."

"They'd have to be daft to believe that," Polly teased.

"Good evening, ladies." An attractive thirtysomething man stood in the open door, hands resting on a well-used tool belt. His name, Mike Dane, was scrawled across the belt in thick black ink.

"Good evening, Mike. Heading home?" Harriet asked.

Her temporary handyman gestured around the grounds of Cobble Hill Farm, which Harriet had inherited from her beloved grandfather. "I was thinking about it, unless there's another task you'd like me to get to before Monday?"

"It's like I told you when I hired you," she assured him. "I'm in no rush on the things I need you to do, with the exception of the gallery's roof." The outbuilding that housed Harold Bailey's studio and gallery had a thatched roof in need of some attention.

Mike nodded. "I took care of that today."

She stared at him. "Already?"

"Yes, ma'am."

"Wow. That was fast." Harriet was impressed. "If you've got your receipts for the materials, I'll write you a check now."

2

He shook his head. "No worries. We can get to that next week."

"Next week it is," she agreed. "Now, go enjoy your weekend."

He tipped his hat at Harriet and then Polly. "You ladies as well." And then he was gone, his long legs quickly carrying him toward the public path along the North Sea.

"I think he should fix lots of things around here." Polly leaned forward in an effort to extend her viewing window. "*Lots* of things."

It was Harriet's turn to laugh. "I thought Van was taking up the bulk of your dance card lately."

At the mention of the sweet but somewhat shy detective constable, Polly's cheeks flushed crimson. "Van Worthington was born with two left feet," she protested. "We tried dancing together once. Suffice it to say, I had to come up with a way to get him off the dance floor without hurting his feelings."

Harriet grinned. "How did you manage that?"

"I feigned thirst and exhaustion."

"And being the gentleman he is, Van immediately ushered you to a seat and got you refreshments." Laughing, Harriet shook her head. "Van has no idea what he's in for with you, does he?"

"He does not."

"Poor bloke," Harriet joked before growing more serious. "Really, though, you two are still enjoying each other's company, right?"

"We are. Very much." Polly headed for her car, calling over her shoulder, "I'll see you tomorrow morning. Have fun de-squeaking Maxwell."

"You know I will." Harriet laughed and shut the door on what had been a successful Friday. Moving to England from Connecticut had been a big change—one she was still adjusting to in many ways.

But, day by day, she was seeing more and more reasons why it had been the right change to make.

Like her deepening friendship with Polly and her growing patient list.

Particularly telling were the peace and contentment she felt in quiet moments.

Harriet smiled down at her dog, letting him into the kitchen. There was no beating her commute to and from work, with the clinic attached to her home. "Well, Maxwell, it's time. Time for both of us to eat, time for you to get your wheels de-squeaked, and time for me to finally start that book I've—"

Her words broke off at a faint but undeniable thump from somewhere above her head, followed by a muted *meow*.

Groaning, she looked back down at Maxwell. "Sorry, buddy. I'll get to you, I promise. But first I need to go upstairs and see what Charlie has gotten herself into."

She took the stairs two at a time to the top and then stopped to listen.

"Charlie," she called. "Curiosity isn't always a wise trait for cats, sweet girl."

The sound of something rolling was followed by a faint jingling, like the sound of a bell.

She made her way toward the attic door she clearly remembered shutting, though it now stood ajar. The clinic cat peered around it at Harriet, a cobweb attached to her ear, which flicked in vain attempts to dislodge it.

"Charlie," Harriet scolded. "How do you keep getting in there?"

4

The patchy calico sat back on her haunches, worked the cobweb free with her front paw, and then darted past Harriet to the stairs.

"Fine. Keep your secrets," she said. "But know that this door and your ability to open it will be added to Mike's list for next week."

She stepped forward to push the door closed but stopped as she remembered the bell sound. Curious, she nudged the door open and felt around on the wall to her left for the light switch. One day, when everything about work and the house and the grounds was exactly the way she wanted it to be, she'd spend time going through the piles and piles of boxes up here. But until then, they'd have to wait.

A quick glance around the unfinished space yielded the answer she sought. On the floor, not more than a few feet away, she saw a small, red plastic ball with a gold bell inside. Harriet picked up the toy then smiled at the curious feline face that appeared beside her at the sound. "Couldn't resist a second look, could you, Charlie-girl?"

The latest in a long line of office cats by that name, Charlie remained silent. She gently pressed a paw against Harriet's leg in a clear request for the ball.

"Let's take this downstairs for you and Maxwell to play with after dinner." She was about to leave when her gaze snagged on the exposed end of an electrical cord. Intrigued, she followed the cord to where it disappeared inside a box in the middle of a stack of other boxes. "I bet you thought that was a snake, didn't you, Charlie?"

She crossed to the stack and pulled back the top flap of the box, intending to wrap the cord up and tuck it inside.

She changed her mind at the sight of the cord's accompanying cassette player and a pile of tapes bearing her grandfather's handwriting.

"What on earth?" she murmured, earning herself a soft meow in response.

She picked up the first cassette and read the label out loud. "'Artie'?" Her thoughts immediately traveled to Grandad's gallery and the painting he'd done of a duck by that name that garnered giggles from youngsters on a daily basis.

She flipped the tape over, found no additional information, and then reached for the next one in the pile. Across the label, Grandad had written MELODY. Again, her thoughts traveled to the gallery and another popular painting, this one of a songbird once owned by fellow White Church Bay resident Meredith Bennett.

Harriet thumbed through the rest of the tapes, the names matching those of animals her grandfather had painted. In fact, she thought nearly every animal that had served as a subject for his talent was represented with a tape. At least all the ones she'd seen in his gallery. She supposed there were other paintings he'd given away and that she'd never seen.

The last one in the pile, however, didn't bear the name of an animal. On that one, her grandfather's writing read MY STORY.

A nudge on her ankle pulled her attention to the floor. The cat was clearly trying to get a point across. "Okay, Charlie. I know it's dinnertime and you want this toy."

She set the tapes back in the box then picked up the whole thing and carried it out of the attic and down the stairs, Charlie traipsing ahead of her.

When she reached the kitchen, she set the box on the floor next to the table, fed the dog and the cat, heated up some soup, and sat down with the box.

She plugged in the cassette player, praying it still worked. Then she took out the tape labeled MY STORY.

She inserted the tape into the machine and pressed play. Her beloved grandfather's voice filled the room.

"My dear wife, Helen, was a questioner. Didn't matter whether she knew you for years or had just met you at the market. She said asking questions and listening to the answers was how families grew closer and strangers became friends. She asked me to make this tape, insisting that someday someone would want my story too, what led me to painting. It's not all that exciting, really, but Helen said it mattered, and I learned early on not to argue with her. So this is for the woman I still feel in my heart every single day."

"Oh, Grandad," Harriet whispered, pressing her hand to her chest. What a gift this tape was.

"I'm not sure whether people realize it, but so many of the animals I've treated over the years have become like family to me. I'm happy to see them when they come in for a checkup, and I worry when they come to me during an illness. Each one has a personality of their own. Some let me see it the moment I first lay eyes on them. Others make me work for it, revealing various bits and pieces over time."

Harriet found herself nodding. She felt the same way.

"From the timid hamster who prefers to eat when no one is watching to the dog who faithfully cared for a litter of orphaned kittens until they were old enough to thrive on their own, each and every animal that has come through my door has left an indelible impression on my soul. I've often found my words inadequate in describing those impressions. Yet when I put paint to canvas, that changes. Instead of trying to put what I see into words that never seem to do an animal justice, I've found that I can *show* what I see. That, my dear Helen, is the story behind my animal paintings."

A series of noises from behind Harriet's chair stole her attention. Parking himself beside her chair, Maxwell leaned against her leg.

"Did you recognize Grandad's voice, boy? He wouldn't have let you squeak at all, would he?" She hit stop on the cassette player. "Let's get your wheels all nice and—"

Her phone rang, cutting her off. After closing time, Polly had the clinic's calls forwarded to Harriet's cell phone. Since she didn't recognize the number, that was clearly what this was, which also meant it was likely an emergency. She answered as she hurried back to the clinic in case she needed anything there. "Hello, this is Dr. Harriet Bailey."

A muffled sob came through the phone. "This is Cindy Summerton. I wouldn't be calling at this hour if it wasn't an emergency. I—I don't know what to do."

"Take a deep breath, Cindy. What's wrong?"

"It's my cat, Nessie," the woman wailed. "She always plays outside in the garden while I'm making supper. It's her routine. But when I shook her can of treats to let her know it was time to come inside, she didn't come."

Harriet's stomach twisted at the words, but she got herself under control. Not too long ago, she'd helped reunite a missing show dog with his owner. Surely this wasn't another missing animal so soon. "I'm sure she'll be back, Cindy. She's probably found something interesting to play with."

"No, the gate was open, and it's not supposed to be."

Something caught Harriet's eye. She crossed the room and stared down at her name in block letters across the top of an envelope that had been shoved under the door. "Did you step outside the gate and shake her treats from there?"

"Of course. But there's no sign of her anywhere."

Harriet picked up the envelope and carried it back to Polly's desk, her curiosity sidelined by the needs of the distraught woman in her ear. "I wouldn't panic yet, Cindy. I really—"

"But, Dr. Bailey, I sent Tarquin out to look for her, and he can't find her either."

Harriet started Polly's computer then pulled up the cat's record. She scrolled until she found the information she wanted. "As I suspected, Nessie is chipped."

"Chipped?" Cindy echoed. "What does that mean?"

"Microchipped. If she's turned in to any shelter or vet office, she'll be scanned and traced back to us here."

"I—I guess that's encouraging."

"It is," Harriet said. "But I suspect Nessie will be sitting outside your garden door first thing tomorrow morning. She'll be hungry and tired from her adventure, but every bit as glad to be home as you will be to have her there."

"And if she's not?"

"We'll cross that bridge if we come to it. Nessie knows she has it good with you, so I'm confident she'll be back." Harriet closed out of Nessie's record and powered off the computer, hoping Cindy couldn't hear that Harriet was trying to convince herself too. But she couldn't ignore the misgivings growing in her mind. "Now, get some rest. When Nessie returns, she'll need lots of cuddles from you, your husband, and your beautiful baby boy. Doctor's orders."

Cindy took a deep breath, sounding calmer. "Thank you, Dr. Bailey."

"Of course. Nessie held a very special place in Grandad's heart, as you well know, along with everyone who's ever stepped inside his gallery and seen his painting of her." Harriet grabbed the envelope. "I'll check with you first thing in the morning. If she's not back by then, we'll send out the cavalry."

"I'd appreciate that," Cindy said, the hitch in her voice lessening. "Good night, Dr. Bailey."

"Good night, Cindy."

Harriet ended the call, opened the envelope, and unfolded the single sheet of paper it contained. Ugly block letters chilled her to the bone.

I HAVE NESSIE.

CHAPTER TWO

"You doing okay?"

Harriet glanced around her computer monitor at the dark-haired receptionist standing in the doorway of her office with two mugs in her hands. "I'm guessing you know, Polly."

She nodded and handed Harriet one of the mugs. "Van and I were debating whether to get vanilla or chocolate ice cream at Galloway's General Store when he got the call."

"I'm sorry. I didn't intend to mess up your evening. I didn't realize they'd send Van."

"No worries. I wasn't terribly excited about the movie he wanted to watch anyway." Polly perched on the edge of Harriet's desk. "So take me through it from the top."

"Cindy Summerton called in a complete panic because Nessie was missing. After she finished with her story, I figured Nessie had simply taken advantage of the open gate to explore beyond her own backyard." Harriet took a sip of her tea. "While I was talking to her, I noticed an envelope under the door that had my name on it. I assumed one of our customers had come by to pay a bill after we'd closed for the day, so I waited to open it until after Cindy and I had hung up. I wish it *had* been a check. Or even a bill."

"So what was it, exactly?" Polly prodded.

"A note that said, 'I have Nessie.'"

"They didn't ask for money or threaten to hurt her if you contacted the police?"

Harriet raised an eyebrow. "You've been watching too many detective shows."

"Isn't that the point of a ransom note?"

Harriet came out from around her desk. "I suppose. But this note didn't ask for anything."

"And why did they put it under our door instead of Cindy's?" Polly mused, trailing Harriet out of the room.

"Your guess is as good as mine on that one."

"Did Van offer any thoughts?"

"None that he's shared with me." Harriet paused in the middle of the reception area and took in the spot where she'd found the note little more than twelve hours earlier. "Haven't you talked to him since the grocery store?"

"He probably thought it was too late to call after he finished up here." Polly took her place behind her desk. "Does Cindy know about the note?"

"It was late by the time Van left, so I don't know if he went straight to Cindy's or if he waited until this morning to talk to her. He recommended that he be the one to break the news to her, and maybe it's cowardly, but I'm all too happy to let him."

Polly powered up her computer. "I can think of one person who might not be terribly crushed if Nessie isn't found. Cindy's dog-loving husband, Tarquin."

Harriet rolled her eyes. "Tarquin Summerton might prefer a dog, but that doesn't mean he'd make Nessie disappear."

"*Might* prefer a dog?" Polly's left eyebrow inched upward.

Harriet held up her hands. "I mean, he was asking about the typical life expectancy of cats the last time he and Cindy came in with Nessie. And, yes, he asked a lot of questions about different breeds of dogs. But to take Nessie and leave a note under my door is a bit of a stretch, don't you think? Especially when he could simply get a dog that's friendly to cats."

"Maybe." Polly nodded in the direction of the parking lot and the fortysomething woman hurrying toward the clinic door with a birdcage in her hands. "Your first patient of the day has arrived."

Harriet took in the woman's nondescript raincoat and slightly tousled hair. "Remind me of the basics?"

Polly tapped a few buttons on her computer's keyboard. "African gray parrot, male, named Wilson. His owner is Theresa Wallace."

"And it's a routine checkup?"

"Actually, she called right before I came into your office. Apparently, Wilson has started plucking out his feathers."

Harriet pulled the door open as the woman reached it. "Theresa Wallace? Welcome. I'm Dr. Harriet Bailey."

"Do you always greet your patients at the front door?" Theresa asked, stepping inside.

"Only the special ones." Harriet smiled at her. "He sure is a pretty fellow."

Theresa unsnapped the front of her raincoat but made no move to take it off. "He won't be for long if he keeps pulling out his feathers."

"I heard about that. Let's take a look, shall we?" Harriet led the way into the first exam room. "How old is Wilson?"

"Four."

"Have you had him the whole time?" she asked, snapping on a pair of gloves.

"Yes."

Harriet unlatched the door of the cage and reached inside. "Has he ever plucked his feathers before?"

"No. Never. And according to my vet back in the States, he's in perfect health."

"Oh? Where in the States are you from?"

"Massachusetts."

"Welcome, fellow Northeasterner. I'm actually from Connecticut." Harriet offered her hand to Wilson, who investigated it then stepped onto it and allowed himself to be removed from the cage. "What brings you here?"

"I'm a novelist," Theresa said. "I felt I'd be more productive working somewhere other than home this time around. So I closed my eyes and pointed at a map of England, and here I am."

"Massachusetts to White Church Bay? That's a big change."

"I've actually spent the last six months in London, but that was for fun. *This* is for work."

"I see." Harriet studied the area with the missing feathers. "And is your feeling proving to be correct?"

"Not yet, but I'm hopeful."

"How long will you be here?"

"Until I finish my book."

With the tip of her finger, Harriet parted the existing feathers in the affected area and compared them with those on the opposite side. "Is it just the two of you?"

"It is."

"Is Wilson a talker?"

"He has a few words he likes to throw out, but he's more into mimicking sounds." Theresa gave a wry smile. "He lets me know if I snore at night. And when I've gotten particularly frustrated. He's got my irritated groan down pat."

Harriet laughed. "When did you get here? To White Church Bay?"

"A little over a week ago," Theresa said, her eyebrows dipping with concern. "But he didn't start acting weird until this morning."

"By weird, you mean the feather-plucking?"

"And the sounds that preceded it. Some clicking and an odd, screechy sound. He's never made those sounds before, and he's never pulled out his feathers."

"African grays are very sensitive birds, and they're often prone to self-plucking as a reaction to stress."

"Our regular vet has always said I take amazing care of him. What stress could he have?"

Harriet gently stroked the top of the parrot's head then set him back in his cage. "Wilson's stress isn't a reflection on you, Ms. Wallace. It's likely a reaction to the change associated with your move here."

"He was in London with me, and when I first came into the country, he handled his quarantine like a champ. If this was about change, wouldn't he have started plucking then?"

"Stress can be caused by many different things," Harriet explained. "It could be the smell of the sea. It could be a different hue in the lights where you're staying. It could be something so subtle you aren't even aware of it."

"The cottage we're renting is less than it was advertised to be. The floors and doors creak, and the wind whistles through the cracks. But I wouldn't think a bird, even one as smart as Wilson, would know the difference," Theresa said. "His cage is the same."

"He might be sensing *your* unhappiness about the place."

Theresa glanced into the cage. "So you're saying I need to fake it better?"

"I'm saying try to keep as much of his routine the same as possible. If he's used to eating at a certain time, be sure to feed him then. If he's used to interacting with you at a certain time each day, try to stay true to that. If he's used to you dancing around the house, dance." Harriet met Theresa's worried expression with the reassurance she knew the woman needed. "Keep things as normal as possible for him, and I'm confident he'll get through the change in one piece. Probably in time for you to go back to the States."

Theresa's answering laugh was void of anything resembling humor or lightness. "That would imply I'll not only start my book but actually finish it as well."

"Isn't that the reason you're here?" Harriet asked.

"It is. But in order to do that, I need to have a plot and characters." Theresa blew out a long breath, earning herself a quick head bob from Wilson. "Instead, I'm wasting hours researching things like poisonous plants, how to flee to another country, the size of the average US jail cell, anonymous email addresses, and miniature cupcakes."

Harriet washed her hands at the exam room sink and quickly dried them with a paper towel. "I would've assumed, based on those first three, that you write police procedurals or mysteries. But with that last one, I'm stumped."

"I'm a romance writer with a thing for dessert."

"Interesting." Harriet crossed to the room's computer, pulled up Wilson's chart, and keyed in a few notes before addressing the bird's owner once again. "Just like we might get stressed when thrust into a new, unexpected situation, I believe Wilson is simply reacting to the change in his surroundings. But I'd like you to bring him back in a week. If he's still plucking, we can run some tests. But truthfully, I'll be surprised if it comes to that."

A tentative smile tugged up one side of Theresa's mouth. "In other words, I should stop using Wilson and his plucked feathers as an excuse not to write?"

"No, you were wise to bring him in." Harriet closed out Wilson's chart and crossed back to the exam table. "Fortunately, I think all he needs is a little time to get used to things."

"A little time," Theresa repeated as she lifted the cage off the table. "For Wilson, I can do that. For my book? Not so much. My deadline looms closer with each passing day."

"I wish I could offer a suggestion that could make things go more smoothly for you in that regard. But I'm a reader, not a writer, and I honestly have no idea how authors like you do what you do. I just know I appreciate the effort and the entertainment that books provide me."

"Music to an author's ear, I'll tell you that." Theresa picked up the cage. "Anyway, thank you. For getting us in first thing this morning and for not making me feel like a lunatic for worrying."

"You know what's normal and what's not for your pet. Paying attention enough to notice when something seems off can make all the difference in the world for their health." Harriet led Theresa out of the room and over to the front desk. "Polly, I'd like to see Wilson back for a follow-up next week."

Polly consulted the calendar on her computer and then glanced up at the bird's owner, undisguised awe evident on her face. "Your last book, *Shore to Shore*? I couldn't put it down. And the ending took my breath away."

Theresa beamed. "Why, thank you."

"Now, for your follow-up. How about next Saturday morning? Same time as today? Will that work?"

"We'll be here. Right, Wilson?"

The bird turned his back on them.

"Give him time," Harriet said, resting a hand on the woman's shoulder. "He's feeling a little sorry for himself at the moment."

Theresa opened the door to the parking lot. "Thank you again, Dr. Bailey. Wilson and I will see you next week." She carried the cage through the door.

"That was really exciting," Polly said, watching her go. "I love her work."

"I didn't realize you knew who she was when she first walked in."

"Because I didn't. She writes as Theresa Wilson, not Theresa Wallace, so the name threw me."

Harriet laughed. "Theresa *Wilson*? As in, the parrot's name?"

"That's it. Anyway, as you were taking her into the exam room, I thought she seemed familiar. So I looked her up and recognized her from her author photo."

"And you really like her books?" Harriet asked.

"I adore her books. You should try them."

"Maybe I should." Harriet leaned across the desk for a peek at the clinic's calendar. "It looks like we have a few minutes before Jane Birtwhistle is due in for Mittens's ear paste. Has Cindy Summerton called by any chance?"

"No." Polly's attention seemed to be on the door rather than Harriet. "Looks to me like she's gone for the more personal touch."

Harriet followed Polly's gaze to the window, where she saw a familiar figure hurrying toward the clinic.

Harriet met her at the door. "Still no sign of Nessie?"

"No! And the police told me about the ransom note." Cindy was even more distraught than the previous night. "Someone *took* Nessie. But why didn't they put the note under *my* door?"

"I don't know, but hopefully we'll be able to figure it out soon." Harriet looked over Cindy's shoulder and saw a car parked in a far corner of the lot. "Polly, I don't understand why Jane would park so far away, but when she comes in with Mittens, please get them settled in the exam room while I finish up here with Cindy."

Polly shook her head. "That's not Jane. It's Mike."

A figure hustled toward the car then paused and glanced at the clinic.

"You're right. It *is* Mike," Harriet said. "But what's he doing here? It's Saturday."

Polly returned the handyman's hesitant wave and then stood as he made his way to the clinic. "Looks like you can ask him that yourself."

"So, you *did* give him a job?"

Harriet turned back to Cindy. "You know Mike?"

"Not really, but when he was going door-to-door asking for work early last week, I suggested he might talk to you. Especially when he said he was a jack-of-all-trades. I figured there are probably odd jobs on a property like this all the time."

Mike came in and drew up short, taking in the three women. "I'm sorry. I don't mean to interrupt. I saw you looking out at me just now, and I figured I should explain why I'm here on a Saturday."

"We were curious," Harriet admitted.

He held up a hammer. "I realized I left this behind not long after I left yesterday. When I did, I came back to search for it, but it was too dark to see. So I came to get it this morning."

"You were here last night? What time?" Harriet asked.

Mike shrugged. "Around six?"

She traded glances with Polly. "Did you see any cars in the parking lot? Anyone moving around outside the clinic?"

"No. Should I have?"

"Just wondering. I'm glad you found your hammer."

"My wallet is too." Mike took a step back. "Anyway, my apologies again for interrupting. Enjoy your day, ladies."

Before he could leave, Cindy blurted, "Have you by any chance seen my Nessie?"

"I'm sorry, but I don't know anyone by that name," Mike said.

"I introduced you to her last weekend when you came to my door." Cindy wiped new tears from her cheeks. "I told you about her connection to Cobble Hill Farm, and I encouraged you to see if you could find work here, remember?"

Mike's expression remained blank. "That part, yes, but I don't recall you talking about a Nessie."

"She's cinnamon and white. Little pink nose. Big yellow eyes."

"Wait. You're talking about your cat? I take it she's missing."

"She was *stolen*!" Cindy insisted. "From my home. By a terrible, horrible person."

"I'm sorry to hear that," Mike said. "Have you put up flyers? So people can be on the lookout for her?"

Cindy's eyes widened. "Flyers? You're right. We should do that. With Nessie's picture and my number."

"It certainly can't hurt," Harried agreed.

"Can you help me?" Cindy begged Polly. "Please?"

Polly began typing. "Of course. And we have her picture on file, so I can include that."

"Could you also include a picture of the painting Dr. Harold did of her?"

"There's a painting of this cat?" Mike asked.

"Yes. Harriet's grandfather found and rescued my precious Nessie when she was little more than the size of my palm. He cared for her for several weeks and then gave her to me in the wake of my mum's passing. We've been inseparable ever since. Or we were." Cindy's voice broke.

"We'll find her, Cindy," Harriet said. "Mike, Nessie's painting was my grandfather's big break in the art world."

Cindy wiped her hand across her eyes. "Something about her sweet little face peeking out from between the rocks where she'd gotten herself stuck resonates with people."

"That and her unique paws," Polly added, still typing.

Mike raised an eyebrow in silent question.

"Nessie is a polydactyl cat," Cindy explained.

"I'm familiar with that term. I had a friend who was a real Ernest Hemingway buff, and I remember him talking about polydactyl cats and their tie to the author."

"The Hemingway cats have six toes on each foot. Nessie has *seven*," Cindy said proudly.

"I'm guessing that's rare?"

"It is."

"Might that have been the painting I heard some bloke offering crazy money for when I was fixing the leak over the gallery's kitchen yesterday?" Mike asked.

"More than likely, yes," Harriet said.

Mike blew out a breath. "I thought he'd lost his mind, offering a thousand pounds for a painting of a cat."

Cindy sucked in a breath then said incredulously, "A thousand pounds?"

Harriet held up her hands. "It doesn't matter how much he offered, because some things are worth more than money. I'm not selling that painting."

"I'd give over every pound I have to get Nessie back," Cindy said. "Every last one."

The printer behind Polly's chair whirred to life, churning out copies of Nessie's picture and description alongside Cindy's name and number.

"I'd be happy to take some of those and put them up around the village," Mike said.

"Yes, please," Cindy said. "The more eyes we have looking, the better chance we have to find her and the horrible person who's taken her."

CHAPTER THREE

With her umbrella now safely in her hands, Harriet rejoined the line slowly snaking its way toward the back of the church. Had she remembered all of her belongings the first time she'd stepped out of her pew, she'd be within a person or two of the arched front doors.

Instead, she was officially last in a long line of churchgoers, but she didn't mind. After all, she enjoyed socializing with such pleasant people. She chatted about the service and the rain beating on the roof with the elderly woman in front of her, biding her time until it was her turn to speak to the pastor.

Familiar faces dotted the line ahead of her, and they smiled when she caught their eyes. She was struck by how little time it had taken for these people to feel like lifelong friends and neighbors.

Her gaze continued down the line until she came to a woman with brown hair that was beginning to gray and a big bag that hung from her shoulder. Doreen Danby was sure to have some of her famous home-baked goods in that bag. Sure enough, she stopped in front of the pastor and offered him what looked like a scone.

To Harriet's surprise, the pastor declined.

Doreen handed the scone to an eager recipient behind her and then stepped out of the church. Harriet made a mental note to see if

Doreen had another of those delicious scones with her when she made it outside herself.

"Good morning, Harriet."

Startled out of her scone-induced reverie, she found herself gazing into the hazel eyes of a man she thought about more than she probably should. "Hi, Will—I mean, Pastor Will."

"You were right the first time."

Harriet hoped her cheeks weren't as red as they suddenly felt. "That was a lovely sermon you gave this morning."

"Thank you." Leaning against the wall at his back, Will scrubbed a hand through his graying brown hair. "Things better at the clinic this week?"

It was so like him to remember and ask about how she was coping with a difficult situation. The previous week, a client had brought in his dog with gastrointestinal distress. Harriet had a sneaking suspicion that the dog had developed food sensitivities, and she'd recommended a blood panel to confirm it. The dog's owner had balked at the cost of the test, as well as the cost of the specialized diet his dog might have to be switched to, and he'd openly accused Harriet of making up a diagnosis to squeeze him for more money.

"I did manage to convince Mr. Renner to do the blood panel, and I was right. Scout is allergic to meat. All meat."

Will's eyes widened. "I didn't know that was a possibility."

"It's not particularly common, but it does exist. It's more frequent for a dog to show a sensitivity to one specific protein, but sometimes their bodies decide all meat is bad. Scout is around a year old, which is the age these sensitivities often reveal themselves.

Fortunately, there are foods and even treats available so that he still gets protein without setting off his allergies."

"How did Mr. Renner take the news?" Will asked.

"Based on the scathing one-star review he posted, I'd say not good. He's still accusing me of price-gouging." Harriet pushed an errant lock of hair behind her ear. "I can understand though. It's hard to accept that a beloved pet has any kind of deficiency, especially when they're young. Scout will be all right—happy even—but I think his owner needs time to adjust to the idea that he'll have to radically change the way his dog eats."

"I'll pray his bad review doesn't hurt your business," Will said. He chuckled. "I'm not sure how well my prayer for Nessie the cat went over with everyone in the congregation today."

"Why? I thought it was sweet. And so would anyone who knows how important Nessie is to Cindy and Tarquin."

Will's laugh echoed in the now-empty church. "I wouldn't necessarily put Tarquin Summerton at cat-fan status, but yes, I'm sure he's distraught if for no other reason than he loves his wife."

"I take it you saw one of the flyers?" Harriet asked.

"I did. It was taped to the door of Galloway's when I stopped to pick up a frozen pizza for dinner, and then again outside Tales & Treasures when I popped in to buy a book."

"I'm glad to know they're out there."

"I actually knew before that though. Cindy called me Friday night and asked me to pray. When I realized Cindy, Tarquin, and Emerson weren't in their usual spot, I knew it was because Nessie is still missing and they're afraid to leave the house in case she comes home."

"And so you did as Cindy asked." Harriet wasn't surprised, as Will occasionally brought strays to the clinic and paid for their care himself. "It appears Nessie didn't leave of her own free will."

"Meaning?"

"I got a note under the clinic door Friday night. I hesitate to call it a ransom note, because it didn't ask for money or anything else, but it's how the police know she was taken rather than just wandered off."

"Did Cindy get one too?"

"No."

"I don't understand."

"Nor do I. Nor do the police." Harriet tightened her grip on her umbrella. "So keep the prayers coming, if you will. They're very much needed."

"I will. And I'll be sure to reach out to Cindy and Tarquin as soon as I get back to the parsonage."

"Thank you, Will." Harriet pressed a hand on her growling stomach. "I'm sorry. I skipped breakfast this morning."

Will laughed. "I can tell."

"I'm surprised you didn't hear it when you turned down that scone from Doreen Danby. Why did you do that, by the way? Don't you know how good they are?"

"Oh, trust me, I'm very aware of how good they are. I'm also aware of how big I'll get if I don't learn to say no every once in a while." Will patted his trim middle.

"Fair enough," she said, only to return her hand to her stomach as yet another gurgle erupted. "Although I sure would like one myself." Harriet knew it was time to leave, but now that she was mere steps from the front door, she suddenly didn't care about scones quite so much. "I should probably go. Enjoy your week, Will."

"You as well, Harriet."

With a quick wave, Harriet stepped onto the front stoop and opened her umbrella against the light but steady rain. She scanned the few remaining chatterers for any sign of Doreen and her bag of scones, but to no avail. Oh well. There would be other times. She hurried toward her old Land Rover.

"Dr. Bailey!"

She turned to the voice. "Ms. Wallace, right?" she asked, extending her right hand to the author.

"Yes, but please call me Theresa."

Harriet smiled. "How is Wilson? Any more plucking?"

"No."

"Is he talking?"

Theresa shook her head. "No, but he's making plenty of those weird sounds. He greeted me first thing this morning with the same clicking sound, the same high-pitched screech, and some yowling. He repeated them over and over again then turned his back to me."

"He'll come around in time," Harriet said. "Moving to a new place can leave people unbalanced at times, and they know what's going on. Wilson doesn't. But as he starts to become familiar with your new place, I'm confident he'll relax."

"I hope so. Because I'm starting to feel real guilt about him, and that's not helping my creativity."

"He'll be fine."

As the rain's pace began to pick up, Theresa pulled her umbrella closer to her. "I wanted to ask if there's been any word on that

27

woman's cat? Nessie, right? I assume she's not back, since Pastor Will prayed for her this morning."

"That's right." Harriet slid her free hand into the pocket of her raincoat and tried not to shiver.

"I also heard about it from the cat's owner when I was leaving your clinic with Wilson yesterday. She said someone took Nessie. Why would someone take a cat?" Theresa frowned. "Aren't there shelters and pet stores around here where people can get one of their own?"

"There are."

"From what I came across yesterday, this cat is rather famous around here."

"What you came across?" Harriet asked.

"What can I say? Research is my favorite form of procrastination."

Harriet laughed. "Nessie has had one or two stories written about her over the years."

"One or two? She was big news for a while, from what I saw. Articles, pictures, letters to the editor even. Clearly, the staff reporters and photographers of the local paper were smitten with the kitten who'd gotten herself stuck between some rocks. And your grandfather rescued her, cared for her, and then gave her to this woman, yes?"

"He did. Cindy's mother was sick for more than a year, and Cindy was her sole caregiver. When her mother finally passed, Cindy had no family left. My grandfather hoped Nessie would be a comfort to her, and he was right. Nessie gave Cindy someone to care for, to talk to, and to love. It proved a true win-win for the two of them."

"And your grandfather went on to paint a picture of Nessie that brings people in droves to some gallery around here?" Theresa asked.

"'In droves' might be an overstatement, but yes, that painting is one of the pieces my grandfather is best known for," Harriet said. "It really seems to speak to people for the story it tells."

"Is that why you became a vet?" Theresa asked. "Because of your grandfather?"

Harriet smiled, at both the question and the memories it evoked. "It certainly didn't hurt. Not when I grew up believing he had the coolest job in the world."

"Very nice. And then, in the last decade or so of his life, he began painting?"

"Wow," Harriet said, impressed. "You really *were* procrastinating, weren't you?"

Theresa laughed. "I was. At least in this case, I have no worries my search topics will put me on some national security watch list."

"Has that happened?" Harriet asked.

"Not to my knowledge. Yet. Do you know what sparked your grandfather's sudden interest in art?"

"He'd always drawn little pictures on my birthday cards when I was growing up. And they were really, really good. He either didn't realize that, or simply didn't allow himself the time to pursue it until the last decade or so of his life."

"I read that his painting of Nessie is worth quite a bit. That's impressive, especially for an artist who came to it later in life. It will likely go higher if news of her abduction gets out."

Harriet stared at the writer. "'Abduction' seems a strong word to use in relation to a cat."

"Maybe, but it's accurate. Anyway, where would I find this gallery?"

"It's on the grounds of Cobble Hill Farm, where you came yesterday with Wilson. It's in the thatched-roof outbuilding near the clinic and is open Monday through Saturday from ten to four."

"If I ever actually make progress on my book and get Wilson settled, I'll have to check it out between writing sessions." Theresa pulled at the arm of her raincoat to reveal a wristwatch. "I should get back to him. I've been gone about an hour."

Harriet pointed over her shoulder at her car. "I'd be happy to drive you home. Especially with all this rain."

"Thank you, but I do some of my best plotting when I walk."

Harriet's answering laugh gave way to another shiver. "Good luck with that."

"Good luck, indeed. Have a great rest of your Sunday, Dr. Bailey."

"You as well. But please, call me Harriet."

She waited until the writer disappeared around the next corner before hurrying the rest of the way to the Land Rover she'd affectionately dubbed "the Beast." Her conversation with Theresa had reminded her of Grandad's tapes, and she was eager to get back to them.

Her stomach grumbled, and she had to chuckle. Her own research would have to wait until after lunch. Some things she just couldn't procrastinate about.

CHAPTER FOUR

Harriet was putting the silverware on the table when she heard her aunt's soft knock at the front door.

"Guess who's here, Maxwell?"

Abandoning his spot beside Harriet's chair, Maxwell scampered down the hallway with Charlie and Harriet close on his wheels. Harriet opened the door to Aunt Jinny, a woman she treasured as both family and friend.

"Well, hello." She embraced her father's sister. "Everything okay?"

Genevieve "Jinny" Garrett handed over a loaf of bread then crouched to greet Maxwell and Charlie. "I'm a bit tired. My day started with stitches for a six-year-old who had a nasty fall. I'd no sooner finished with him when I got a call from another patient who was feeling poorly."

"So that's why I didn't see you in church this morning." Harriet led the way into the kitchen. "I imagine you're exhausted."

Nodding, Aunt Jinny pulled out her chair at the table and flopped down. "I am. But this will perk me up, I'm sure."

Harriet began slicing the meat loaf. "Good, because I have something to show you and a million questions to ask once we've eaten."

"I'm assuming it has to do with all of that?" Her aunt gestured to the box of cassettes.

"Yes. They're recordings of Grandad talking about stuff."

"What kind of stuff?"

Harriet transferred the meat loaf to a serving plate and carried it to the table then added bowls of mashed potatoes and corn, as well as a gravy boat. "One of them talks about why he started painting, because he says Gran would have wanted him to share that."

Aunt Jinny chuckled. "Mum *did* like to know the why of things."

Harriet came to stand beside her aunt and the box. "These tapes and getting to hear Grandad's voice were all I could think about on the drive home from church today."

"I don't blame you. What are the rest of them?"

"Based on how he labeled them, Grandad seems to have made tapes for some of his animal paintings. I listened to the one about his story, and then the one about Cindy Summerton's cat, Nessie."

"I'm surprised you only listened to two."

"I wanted to hear his voice, yes, but with Nessie missing, I also—"

Aunt Jinny's eyes snapped from the tape to Harriet. "Nessie is *missing*? How? When?"

"Since late Friday afternoon. Someone took her from Cindy's garden. Or at least, that's what the note I got under the clinic door implies. And Van agreed when he responded to my police call."

Aunt Jinny's eyes narrowed. "And I'm just now hearing about this?"

"By the time Van left, it was late and I didn't want to wake you. Then, with work on Saturday, and how tired I was afterward, I figured I'd tell you today."

"What did the note say?"

"'I have Nessie.'"

"You can't be serious. There were no clues or anything? And there's been no sign of her since?"

"Nothing."

Aunt Jinny winced. "Cindy must be beside herself."

"She is," Harriet said. "But Polly made flyers, and Mike—our temporary handyman—put them up around town."

"Good thinking. Hopefully the right person will see them and Nessie will be returned to Cindy, safe and sound."

"I'll admit, when Cindy first called Friday night, I was sure curiosity had led Nessie astray," Harriet said. "But that note changed everything."

"But why would someone take her? And why would they tell you and not Cindy?"

"I've been thinking about that all day, and the only thing that makes sense to me is that it's someone who knows that I'm Nessie's vet, and they didn't want to get caught leaving a note at Cindy's house. It was after hours when I found it in the clinic where it had been shoved under the door." Harriet tapped the tape devoted to Nessie's painting, recalling everything she'd learned from it since returning home from church. "Did you know that it wasn't Grandad who found Nessie but another man by the name of Felix?"

Aunt Jinny made a face. "That would be Felix Burton."

"Right. But after I listened to Grandad talk about that day, I went online and pulled up the article written about Nessie's rescue. It doesn't mention this other man at all. Did Grandad take credit for what Felix did?"

"Not at all. Felix spotted her while crossing the footbridge. He reached out to Dad, who did the actual rescuing. Once he freed her, he brought her here, where he bottle-fed her for the next six weeks, keeping her with him every moment to make sure she was okay."

"That part doesn't surprise me. Let's continue this over dinner before it gets cold." The two of them settled at the kitchen table, and after Harriet said grace, they began passing food back and forth.

Aunt Jinny took a bite of the meat loaf. "This is my mum's recipe, isn't it?"

"It is. I found it a week or so ago and knew I had to make it for you the first chance I got."

"Thank you, dear. It's perfect." Aunt Jinny took another bite and closed her eyes.

Harriet managed a genuine smile in spite of the questions rattling around in her mind. "I feel like I found a way to include both Gran and Grandad in my day. It's been really nice."

"What a lovely thought."

They both cleaned their plates. Leaning back against her chair, Aunt Jinny released a happy sigh. "That was delicious, Harriet. Thank you."

"You're very welcome."

Aunt Jinny glanced at the dog beside her feet. "I don't think I've heard Maxwell squeaking at all."

Harriet took a sip of water. "I oiled his wheels after work on Friday."

"Well done. Dad would be proud."

"I'm glad to hear it." Harriet got back to the matter at hand. "So, I have to ask. Why the face when I mentioned Felix?"

"Because he wasn't a very nice man. Especially to Dad."

Harriet gaped at her. "*Everyone* loved Grandad."

"Felix was the one exception."

"How?" Harriet repeated. "Why? And does he still live in White Church Bay?"

"He passed away at the beginning of the year, just a little while before you moved here, in fact."

"Would I have met him during one of my visits as a kid?"

Aunt Jinny took a sip of water. "Unlikely. They weren't friends, though Dad tried."

"What was Felix's issue with Grandad?" Harriet asked.

"I couldn't say how it started, but over the last decade or so, Felix's dislike boiled down to one simple fact—that Dad was liked by everyone in White Church Bay."

"And Felix wasn't, I take it?"

Aunt Jinny snorted. "Not particularly. But that was because of his own doing, not Dad's as he liked to claim. Felix blamed everything that didn't go his way on Dad. He was convinced that Harold Bailey had taken everything from him, and he'd say so to anyone who'd listen."

"What did he think Grandad had taken?"

"Throughout their boyhood, Felix considered himself in competition with Dad, but Dad always topped him in marks, extracurriculars, you name it. Apparently, Felix even had an eye for Mum when they were in school. But Mum liked Dad, and Dad liked Mum. For Felix, that was Dad winning. Again."

"But Grandad never would have rubbed it in his face or anything."

"Of course not, but Felix saw him as competition to the success he felt should be handed to him rather than earned. Which, as you know, was not the way your grandfather was. He worked hard for everything he had and truly appreciated his many blessings."

Harriet gave a low whistle, unable to imagine nursing such a grudge for so long. "Did Felix eventually get married? Have a family? Have a job or run a business?"

"He did. He married a woman named Phyllis. I went to school with their daughter, Michelle. She didn't like me."

"Because of her father?" Harriet asked.

Aunt Jinny shrugged. "She was raised to dislike anyone with the last name Bailey."

"Does she dislike you even now?"

Aunt Jinny gathered her plate, silverware, and napkin and pushed back from the table. "She and her Scottish husband moved to Glasgow after their wedding, and I haven't seen her since. I've heard she had a daughter about the same time I had Anthony, and maybe a son a year or so later. But that's it. I like to think, after all this time, she has better things to think about than me."

"She didn't come back to White Church Bay for her father's funeral?"

"There was no funeral. Not in White Church Bay anyway. I heard that his ashes were shipped to her in Scotland. It didn't really surprise me that they didn't have a funeral here though. It would've been poorly attended, I'm afraid."

Aunt Jinny carried her dishes to the sink and started the hot water. "So, as you heard on the tape, Felix is the one who found Nessie under the bridge, though none of the articles or reports about it mentioned

36

him. That's because Dad did the work of rescuing and nurturing her, but Felix was furious nonetheless. He just got angrier when the painting of Nessie brought Dad even more attention. He felt that Dad, once again, had stolen something that should've been his."

"Grandad didn't write the articles and reports," Harriet protested as she rose to help with the dishes.

"I know that, and you know that, but, in Felix's eyes, Dad only knew to rescue Nessie because of him. All of the attention he received from the rescue and the painting wouldn't have existed if Felix hadn't found Nessie."

Harriet frowned. "By 'found,' you mean saw her and got word to Grandad?"

Nodding, Aunt Jinny rinsed a plate and handed it to Harriet to dry. "The *Whitby Gazette* got so many letters asking about Nessie after that first story that they did several follow-ups. They published photos of Dad bottle-feeding her in a rocking chair, of her sleeping on his chest, of her following him around the clinic. There was another article when he gave her to Cindy. In it, Cindy talked about how Dad giving her Nessie rescued her from a bad place after her mother's death. It was a very moving piece, as I recall."

"And then the paper wrote about Grandad again when he painted his picture of Nessie," Harriet said.

"Correct. That particular story went beyond the *Whitby Gazette*. It was picked up by a news station on the telly, an art magazine or two, a few papers in neighboring villages, et cetera."

"Did Felix try to cause trouble during any of that?" Harriet asked.

"Dad always gave Felix credit for being the one who first spotted Nessie. Mentioned it to every reporter and photographer he spoke to. But the story they wanted was Dad and Nessie. Dad pulled her out of the rocks. Dad brought her back here, to the house. Dad fed her and cared for her. Dad gave her to Cindy. Dad painted her picture. There was no changing that."

Harriet dried and put away the gravy boat. "Do you think Felix wanted Grandad to say *he'd* done all those things even though he hadn't?"

"I don't know."

"Perhaps Felix was upset that Grandad gave Nessie to Cindy instead of him."

"Felix didn't want Nessie. He was allergic to cats, for one thing, and he told everyone and anyone who would listen that he didn't like animals."

"Why?" Harriet asked. "Because Grandad loved them?"

"Quite likely. Anyway, enough about Felix Burton and ancient history. I want to talk about Nessie and the note. I agree with you about her connection to the clinic being why the note came to you."

Harriet finished putting away the silverware. "What doesn't make sense is why someone would take her at all. She's a cat."

"I'm sure the police will figure it out," Aunt Jinny said.

"I hope you're right."

"Can we listen to a few of Dad's tapes? It would be a nice cap on a trying day for me and a trying weekend for you."

"We can listen to all of them if you'd like." Harriet picked up the box.

"I wish I could." Aunt Jinny yawned as she trailed Harriet into the living room. "But with a full roster of patients tomorrow, I really should get some shut-eye. Besides, I think it would be nice to stretch them out. It'll give me something to look forward to."

"Makes sense. Is it okay with you if I listen to the rest on my own? It's a good distraction for me right now."

"Please do. But is everything okay, aside from this stuff with Nessie?"

"I'm upset about Scout's diagnosis and his owner's reaction to it."

"Is he still giving you a hard time?"

"I called and tried to talk to him Friday morning, but he didn't want to hear from me. So I had Polly email him the blood panel report."

"Did that help?"

"Based on the review he went on to post about me, I'd say no."

"Give it time, Harriet," Aunt Jinny said. "He'll come around."

Harriet inserted the first tape into the player. "I'm also missing Grandad, you know? Some days more than others."

"I feel the same." Aunt Jinny pulled Harriet in for a hug. "I imagine you're also missing Connecticut a little too, aren't you?"

Harriet rested her cheek against Aunt Jinny's. "I miss Mom and Dad, for sure. And knowing that Mom is worried about me being so far from home is hard too. I'm figuring it all out, slowly but surely. Driving on the left side, learning the different expressions, meeting people, all of it. And I'm starting to earn the trust and respect of Grandad's patients and their owners."

"Good." Aunt Jinny released her. "I knew everyone would come to love you as they did Dad."

Harriet laughed. "I wouldn't go that far. But I'm making progress. Little by little."

"And you like living here?" Aunt Jinny asked, motioning at the house around them. "Both on Cobble Hill Farm and in White Church Bay?"

"I do. Very much."

"You and Polly have really hit it off," Aunt Jinny mused.

"We have. She's great fun."

"I hear she's dating Van."

"She is."

"Is it exclusive?" Aunt Jinny asked.

"I believe it is."

Aunt Jinny looked closely at Harriet. "And you? Have you gone on any dates? Met any nice young men?"

"I've met lots of nice people, Aunt Jinny."

"Pastor Will is single."

She did her best to hold back the smile born on the mere mention of the kindhearted man. "There are a few single men in White Church Bay, Aunt Jinny. But I'm not ready to dip my toes into that pool again yet."

Aunt Jinny took her hand. "Your engagement in Connecticut ended because Dustin wasn't the right man for you, Harriet. But that doesn't mean the right one isn't out there."

She swallowed against the lump in her throat. "Thanks, Aunt Jinny. I'm not quite ready to search for him."

"Okay. But remember, if you ever need to talk, I'm right across the way."

"I know. You're the best. And now, should we make Gran happy and let Grandad tell us why he started painting?"

"A why you already know."

"True. But I'm more than happy to hear him tell it all over again. Like I'll be happy to hear about his painting of Nessie again." Harriet set a box of tissues beside her aunt. "Are you ready?"

At Aunt Jinny's answering nod, Harriet pressed play.

41

CHAPTER FIVE

On Monday morning, Harriet stepped into the clinic, greeted Polly, and stopped dead in her tracks.

"Do we have some sort of scheduling error?" she asked, pointing to the window and the full parking lot beyond. "This waiting room isn't big enough for that many people and their pets."

Polly tapped her finger on the day's printed schedule. "Two of those cars are for us, max. The rest are here to visit the gallery."

"The gallery doesn't open for another two hours."

Polly rose from her chair, crossed to the coffee maker in the corner of the reception area, and poured the steaming hot liquid into Harriet's favorite mug. "I imagine they want to be closer to the front of a queue I suspect is only going to grow as the day goes on."

Harriet accepted the coffee, thanked her friend, and peered toward the gallery entrance. Sure enough, a line already waited. On a drizzly November morning.

"Is there some sort of sale I don't know about?" she asked.

"No. From what I was able to gather on my way in, people are champing at the bit to help with Nessie." Polly tucked a purple strand of her otherwise dark hair behind her ear. "Others are probably just curious."

"But why are they here instead of at Cindy's?"

Polly made her way back to her desk chair. "You didn't watch the news last night, did you?"

"No. Aunt Jinny came for supper, we had a little much-needed time with Grandad, and then I took a book to bed."

"How on earth did you spend time with your grandfather?" Polly asked.

"I didn't tell you about the cassette tapes Grandad made, did I? I'm sorry. Things have been so crazy. I found a bunch of them in the attic after work on Friday. They're of Grandad talking about his art. I listened to the first one that talks about why he started painting, and then on Sunday, I listened to the one he did about Nessie's painting. I played them again for Aunt Jinny after dinner last night,"

"And there are more besides those?"

"Many more."

"And you didn't listen to the rest after she left?" Polly asked.

"No. Maybe it's silly, but I want to spread them out a little so I can make my time with him last a little longer."

"It's not silly at all. Was it good to hear his voice?" Polly asked.

"It was *wonderful*. Absolutely wonderful."

"Could I hear them one day?"

"Of course. So Nessie was on television?" Harriet asked.

"She was. On the local segment that reporter, Candace Moore, does a few times a week."

"I know Nessie was taken, but this is White Church Bay. When Petey went missing last month, it didn't get much press, and he's a show dog. How did this reporter find out about Nessie?"

"My guess is that someone called Candace and told her. And my top suspect is in the parking lot right now."

Harriet spotted a familiar figure removing a toddler from a car seat. "You think Cindy called a television news reporter?"

"She tells everyone she meets about her seven-toed polydactyl cat and how she came to get her. Is it really that much of a stretch?"

Harriet smiled. "True."

Polly readied herself for the role of clinic greeter as their eight o'clock—a Saint Bernard and her owner—approached the door. A chill swept into the room as the Saint Bernard's owner opened the door and followed the leashed dog into the waiting area.

"Good morning, Mr. Armstrong. Good morning, Sadie." Polly stepped out from behind her desk. "We're happy you're here."

Lowering her fingers into sniff range, Harriet waited for Sadie to deem her a friend and then squatted down to the dog's eye level. "Hello, Sadie. Aren't you the prettiest girl? Such beautiful fur. And your chart says you just had a birthday. Polly, don't we give out biscuits for that?"

"We sure do, Doc," Polly said with a grin.

Sadie accepted the dog biscuit with a tail wag.

Harriet straightened and extended her hand to the man at the end of Sadie's leash. "Hello, Mr. Armstrong. I'm Dr. Harriet Bailey. Dr. Harold Bailey was my grandfather, as I'm sure Polly told you when you scheduled Sadie's annual checkup."

"I would've known you were Doc Bailey's kin even if she hadn't. You have the same kindness in your eyes. I suspect the animals love you the way they always did your grandfather. I can already tell from the way you've taken to Sadie."

"Thank you, Mr. Armstrong. That is certainly high praise."

"Andy. Please." He glanced over his shoulder as a rush of cold air preceded Cindy and her son into the clinic. "Hello. You're the woman from the telly last night. The one with the stolen cat."

Cindy pursed her lips and nodded. "Her name is Nessie."

"I'm guessing she hasn't been found yet?" Andy asked gently.

Cindy swallowed hard. "No."

"I'm sorry."

"I just don't understand who would take her, or why no one has called saying they've spotted her with her captor. And I thought that chip was supposed to tell us where she was."

"It will—if Nessie is found and brought to a clinic or humane society. They'll check her for a chip, and it'll tie her back to us here," Harriet explained.

"And that hasn't happened?" Cindy asked.

"Not yet, no. I'm sorry."

"Then we should probably return home in case someone recognizes her from the flyer and calls me. Or should we drive around and search for her that way? But what if we do that and someone finds her and takes her to our house, but we're not there?" Cindy ran her free hand over her face. "I don't even know what I should be doing."

"Many of us who didn't know about Nessie do now," Andy told her. "Between the flyers and the news story last night, more people are on the lookout."

Polly stepped out from behind her desk with Sadie's chart. "Mr. Armstrong is right, Cindy. You talking to Candace Moore last night was brilliant. All those people lined up outside the gallery two hours before it opens are here because of that news story. They want Nessie to be found and returned to you, safe and sound."

Cindy pointed toward the window and the heavy fog beginning to roll in. "But she's out there somewhere, not in the gallery."

Suddenly, the toddler in Cindy's arms squealed, "Doggy!"

"Yes, Emerson, the man has a doggy. But you miss *Nessie* very much, don't you?" Cindy began bouncing the toddler. "Nessie, our kitty?"

Emerson pointed at Sadie. "Doggy!"

Cindy's attempt at a smile fell short. "The longer Nessie is gone, the more Emerson's memory of her seems to be fading. It's breaking *my* heart, if not Tarquin's."

"Oh, Cindy, Tarquin knows how important Nessie is to you." Polly gave Cindy a tissue from the box on her desk. "I'm sure he's missing her too."

Cindy dabbed at the tears beginning to work their way down her round face. "He knows I'm upset, and he takes no joy in that, of course, but I know he's looking ahead. Thinking about what if we don't get Nessie back?" Her voice cracked on the last few words.

Harriet laid a hand on her arm, unable to give her an answer.

Cindy lowered her tissue, anguish etched on her face. "Not more than twenty-four hours before Nessie was taken, Tarquin was trying to talk me into getting a dog. He went on and on about some litter of puppies some bloke in the pub was trying to find homes for."

"Tarquin grew up with dogs. It makes sense that he holds a soft spot for them," Polly said.

"Not just a soft spot. He's chosen the one he wants and even has a name picked out for it, Sherlock. Because he knows how I love to read mysteries, and he's hoping I'll fall for the name and allow the puppy into the house. But I won't. Nessie was there for me after Mum died and gave me a reason to go on. Without her, I might not have ever left the house to meet Tarquin, let alone marry him. And if we hadn't met and married, there would be no Emerson."

The toddler barely flinched at the sound of his name. Instead, he flung himself over Cindy's arm for a better view of Sadie, prompting his mom to gently pull him upright as she continued.

"I told Tarquin that as long as Nessie was in our home, there would be no dog terrorizing her, no matter how smartly named. But if she doesn't come back, Tarquin is going to push for that dog." Cindy bit her lip then took a deep breath and gave a trembling smile. "Anyway, Emerson and I should go. But, Harriet, if you hear anything about Nessie, you'll call me right away, won't you?"

Harriet met and held Cindy's worried gaze. "You have my word, Cindy."

CHAPTER SIX

Harriet tugged the purple bedazzled leash from the hook beside the door and shook it at Polly. "If I didn't already know who left this behind, I'd think it was yours."

"Because it's colorful and fun?" Polly shut down the computer, pushed back from her desk, and grabbed her empty lunch tote. "Just like me?"

"Exactly."

"Will you be okay if I head out?" Polly asked.

"Why wouldn't I be?"

Her friend raised an eyebrow. "You've been rather broodish all day."

Harriet frowned. "How have I been 'broodish'?"

"After every appointment, you've gone back into your office rather than chat with me. And when I asked if you wanted a cuppa a while ago, all I got was a nod. The same nod I got when I put it on your desk."

"I'm sorry, Polly. I didn't mean to be rude."

"I know. It's why I chose the word *broodish*. I imagine it's because of the latest review from Dale Renner."

Harriet groaned. "He posted another one? What did he say this time?"

48

"It doesn't really matter."

"In other words, he claimed I'm a liar and a cheat."

"Pretty much." Polly meticulously folded her empty lunch tote and shoved it into her purse. "But he's still the only one-star rating we have."

"No, that makes three now. Two for me, and one for the clinic."

"Yes, but all written by the same person. And surrounded by a sea of four and five stars." Polly's face grew somber. "And Scout's food allergy is hardly your fault. The blood panel report spelled that out. Mr. Renner should be thanking his lucky stars that you knew to check for that and that his dog is alive during a time when there's a good solution for the problem."

"A lot of people who see his review probably don't know that," Harriet reminded Polly. "They'll believe him that I make up reasons to charge my clients more money."

"I could reply to the review and tell readers the truth."

"Mr. Renner is upset. Let's give him some time and hope that our many good reviews compensate for his negative ones. He may come around eventually."

"You're the boss," Polly said. "So if it's not this latest review that has you distracted, what is it?"

"I keep thinking about the conversation with Cindy this morning," Harriet said.

"Specifically, the part about Tarquin?"

Harriet grimaced. "I thought you were crazy when you first suggested Tarquin as a possible suspect in Nessie's disappearance. But after what she said about him not only picking out a certain dog but also naming it, I'm not so sure."

49

"And I don't think we're alone. Did you catch the expression on Mr. Armstrong's face? Clearly the possibility entered his mind as well."

"I did." Harriet plucked a more sedate leash from the next hook. "Yet you and I both know how crazy Tarquin is about Cindy. At least it seems that way every time I see them together."

"It does." Polly crossed to the door and opened it to the gray, late afternoon day and the full parking lot. "It's getting cold out. You sure you don't want me to take our two overnight guests for a walk before I head out?"

Harriet shooed Polly onto the sidewalk. "I've got it. I don't want you to keep Van waiting."

"I didn't say I was seeing Van."

"Not out loud. The number of times you've fussed with your hair in the last two minutes has told me that."

Polly grinned. "I have a hankering for fish and chips. So does Van. It's only polite to pick up an extra order at Cliffside Chippy and drop it off at the station on my way home."

"If you're going to the station, will you see if they've got any leads on who took Nessie?"

"I'll try, but I can't promise Van will tell me anything."

"Thanks," Harriet said. "I know it's their job to find Nessie and the person who took her. But the note telling us she was taken rather than simply missing was pushed under *my* door. It makes me feel as if I have a part in this."

"I get that. If I hear anything, I'll let you know tomorrow morning."

Harriet nodded. "Sounds like a plan. Now go have fun."

Polly had no sooner stepped out the door than Harriet's cell phone rang. She saw the name on the screen and answered immediately.

"Hello, Ida," Harriet greeted the gallery manager. "Need some help moving folks toward the exit?"

"Actually, if it's okay with you, I was wondering if we could stay open a little longer than normal today," Ida Winslow replied. "It doesn't feel right to make people leave when they've been waiting so long. Especially when my only plan for the evening is to watch the telly."

"It's four o'clock, Ida. Our closing time is clearly posted inside the gallery and on the website." Harriet headed for the barn, where her boarders waited for their evening walk.

"I know, but I don't mind staying. Truly."

Harriet counted the people in line for the gallery as she passed. "There are still thirteen people out here, on top of however many are already inside with you. Are you sure?"

"Definitely. Those last few who've been waiting outside in the cold deserve to see the painting they've come to see."

"All of these people are here to see Grandad's painting of Nessie?" Harriet asked. "She was little more than a week or two old in Grandad's painting. It's been six years since then."

"I guess it's easier to empathize with her plight now because of her plight then," Ida said. "People are upset that she was taken, and they want to help find her. In fact, the people at the front of the line this morning were talking about setting up search parties."

Harriet stopped outside the barn, opened the large door, and smiled at the barked greetings she received in return. "I suppose I've lived here long enough that I shouldn't be surprised so many people care."

"I also have two sealed envelopes I've been asked to give you regarding Nessie's painting."

Harriet had frequently received offers for her grandfather's work that way. "Did you tell them it's not for sale?"

"Of course," Ida said. "But they both insisted I give you their envelope anyway. One was a man who expressed confidence that you would feel differently when you saw his offer."

Harriet let the boarders out of their kennels and snapped the leashes to their collars. "He could offer the universe, but that painting is not for sale, now or ever."

"So should I throw the envelopes away?"

"No, you can leave them on the counter for me when you close up. I'll review them, if for no other reason than to know exactly what I'm refusing. Then I'll throw them out."

"Okay. Oh, you might want to empty the donation box while you're here."

"Really? I just did that last night." Admission to the gallery was free, but most people were generous, and Harriet usually emptied the donation box once a week or so.

"I know, but the box is stuffed full today."

"What a marvelous surprise!"

"Yes indeed. Ah, it looks like some are leaving, so I can let some more in."

"You're really okay staying past your normal time? I can take over once I finish walking my boarders." Harriet let the two dogs lead her around the back garden based on the smells they found most appealing. One was a high-energy Labrador named Murphy, the other a rather aloof poodle named Princess.

"Don't worry about it. I love how many people are eager to see Doc Bailey's paintings. I only wish your grandfather could be here. I suspect he'd have gotten a kick out of the questions I've been asked."

"What kind of questions?" Harriet asked.

"How he came to find Nessie between those rocks and whether she bit him. Why he named her Nessie." Ida sighed. "I did my best to answer what I could, but I'm not Harold Bailey. I can't know all of his whys."

Harriet's eyes opened wide as an idea struck her. "What if we could share his whys, and from his own mouth to boot?"

Ida's sharp intake of air was audible. "Don't tease me. That's not possible."

"More possible than you know. I might need your help and Aunt Jinny's, but I think there might be a way to make that happen." She laughed, her mind filling with the idea of a self-guided tour of the gallery, narrated by Grandad himself. "And it probably wouldn't be all that difficult, especially if the donation box is as full as you say."

CHAPTER SEVEN

"Excuse me, Doc?" Harriet smiled at the handyman standing in her office doorway. "Hey, Mike. Happy Tuesday. Come on in. What can I do for you?"

He gestured toward the open door. "I planned to tell Polly out at her desk, but with back-to-back calls she needed to address, she waved me straight in. Sorry about that."

"We hit the ground running the moment we opened this morning. However, if you have a question or a problem, I'd rather you come straight to me unless I'm with a patient. What's on your mind?"

"I was on my way to my car to grab my lunch when I saw the van pull in and figured I should tell you she was here. The news reporter who did the story on Nessie Sunday night, Candace something or other."

Harriet gaped at him. "Why would she be here?"

"I don't know."

"Excuse me for a second." Harriet dashed into the reception area, the handyman on her heels. "Polly, have we heard from Cindy this morning?"

"Three times so far."

"There haven't been any negative developments regarding Nessie, have there?"

"No, but I pumped Van for any information he could give me when I dropped off his fish and chips last night. I intended to fill you in this morning, but this is the first breather I've had."

"What did he tell you?" Harriet prompted.

"They didn't get any prints from the note except yours, which they have on file from previous cases you've worked on. Which means whoever slid it under our door was probably wearing gloves. The leading theory about why we got the note seems to be that the perpetrator felt it would be safer to leave the note here rather than increase the risk of being seen by Cindy."

"But why bring it here as opposed to, say, her neighbor's porch or something?" Harriet asked.

"Because anyone who's ever met Cindy has heard about Nessie's connection to Doc Bailey and this place," Polly said. "Right, Mike?"

"What do you mean?" he asked.

"Cindy is the one who suggested you come here when you were looking for work, right?"

He hesitated then gave a slow nod. "She did. When I told her I was good with my hands, she thought maybe you'd have something for me. Thankfully, she was right."

"And you met Nessie when you stopped at her house, right?"

"Yes, though I didn't remember that until she said it the other day. I stopped at a lot of houses that day. And I think that reporter is about ready."

Sure enough, a thickly built man of about fifty stepped out from behind a van in the parking area with a camera on his shoulder. Seconds later, a blond woman exited the passenger side of the vehicle and smoothed her gray tailored skirt.

"That's Candace Moore," Polly said, clearly stunned.

The reporter and cameraman started toward the clinic.

"What do I say?" Harriet wondered aloud.

The handyman shrugged. "Depends on what they want."

"If they want to know our thoughts on what happened to Nessie, maybe we don't tell them," Polly added. "Lest we send Cindy into more of a tizzy than she already is."

"You mean about her husband?" Harriet asked.

Mike drew back. "You think her husband took her cat?"

Before Harriet could respond, the clinic door swung open and Candace Moore breezed in.

"We're looking for Dr. Harriet Bailey," the reporter announced.

Polly nudged Harriet forward. "You've found her. She's the clinic veterinarian."

The reporter's bright blue eyes took in Harriet from head to toe. "Right. You're the one who got the farm and the house and the clinic when the original Dr. Bailey passed."

"Yes, he left them to me. How can I help you?"

The news reporter reached into her skirt pocket, pulled out a cream-colored card, and thrust it at Harriet. "Candace Moore, local segment reporter for YTV, and this is Doug, my cameraman. I did a piece on the Sunday evening newscast about a cat from White Church Bay that was taken from her yard."

"Nessie," Harriet said.

"Right. I understand from her owner that a note was left under your door from the person responsible for the cat's disappearance."

Harriet traded glances with Polly. "Yes."

"I also understand there was no demand of any kind."

"That's right."

"I've been told Nessie was a polydactyl cat, and that's unusual?" Candace prodded.

"It's unusual, yes. But not unheard of." Harriet crossed her arms in front of her chest and went into lecture mode. "The American novelist Ernest Hemingway was given a polydactyl cat by a ship's captain in the 1930s and named her Snow White. Now, nearly a hundred years later, the grounds of his home and museum in Key West, Florida, are inhabited by descendants of that same cat, with all of them containing the polydactyl gene in their DNA and half of them having the actual polydactyl trait."

"Polydactyl refers to the number of toes, correct?"

"Right. The Hemingway cats are six-toed polydactyls. Nessie is actually rarer as she has seven toes on each paw."

"Do you think that played a part in her abduction?"

Harriet considered then replied, "I hadn't thought about it, to be honest, but I can't rule it out."

"Can I see the note?" Candace asked.

"I'm sorry, but I gave it to the police."

"Certainly. Now, I understand that the painting your grandfather did of Nessie truly made his career."

"It was one of his most acclaimed paintings, and it launched his work into notoriety," Harriet corrected. "But his main career was caring for animals in White Church Bay as the local veterinarian."

"And he was beloved by all," Polly added, earning herself a raised eyebrow from Candace.

"Regardless of who thought what about him and whether painting was his official career or not, it's quite clear that his work speaks to people." Candace pulled out a cell phone.

"It does," Harriet agreed. "In fact, that's something we hear often. But it was his work with animals as a veterinarian that he treasured—"

Candace tapped her French-manicured nails on the phone's screen a few times then flipped it for Harriet to see. "Half a dozen viewers sent me photos like this yesterday evening."

Harriet studied the photos Candace swiped through. Each one was of people standing in line at Cobble Hill Farm. "Those were taken out there on the walkway leading to the gallery."

"Where people lined up all day long to see your grandfather's work. Or, more specifically, the painting he did of the stolen cat everyone is talking about."

"Thanks to your story the other night," Polly said.

"Just doing my job." Candace tossed her hair over her shoulder. "Which is to pursue the story. Clearly, based on these pictures I was sent, I followed the correct path, much like the reporters who first introduced Nessie to the world six years ago."

Harriet took in the current photo on Candace's phone as the reason for the reporter's presence took shape in her thoughts. "If you're wanting to do a follow-up on Nessie and the attention her disappearance has attracted, our gallery manager, Ida Winslow, may be able to offer some insight. I know she spoke to many guests yesterday who followed up their viewing of Nessie's painting with inquiries about what they could do to help find her."

"Actually, I'm not here about Nessie's abduction so much as I am about her painting."

"I see." Harriet gestured to the door. "Would you like to view it in person?"

"Very much."

"Great. I can take you over to the gallery—"

"Actually, boss, I think your next appointment just pulled in, but I'd be happy to run Candace and Doug over to the gallery if that'll help," Polly offered. The clinic phone rang, and she scowled at it. "If that thing ever stops ringing anyway."

"I can take them over."

Harriet stared at the handyman. "Really, Mike? It's hardly within your job description."

He met her gaze. "Not a problem. I'd be happy to walk them over to the gallery while you and Polly take care of things in here."

"Thank you, Mike. That would be great." She turned back to the reporter and cameraman. "If you have any questions Ida is unable to answer, I'm here in the clinic until four. I can see you in between patients."

Candace put her phone away then motioned toward the camera on Doug's shoulder. "Actually, there is *one* question I suspect is better suited for you than the gallery manager, if I may."

Harriet drew back. "On camera?"

"Not live, but yes. Is that a problem?" Candace asked.

"No." Harriet squared her shoulders. "Ask what you'd like."

Doug signaled to Candace, and she began. "Of all the paintings done by your late grandfather, Dr. Harold Bailey, the one of Nessie has been one of the most sought after. Do you think that's because of her seven-toed paws?"

"There's plenty of allure in the image of this tiny little kitten with catcher's mitts for paws. But I think it's more about what Nessie's story says about fear, loneliness, and hope. Hope that things will be okay and love will win out in the end, the way it did for Nessie," Harriet said.

"For six years anyway," Candace said into the camera. "Desperate to find a happy ending for a beloved story that's become tragic once again, people have been flocking to see the late artist's painting of the missing Nessie—on the grounds of the very estate where the once frightened kitten found real hope thanks to Dr. Bailey himself."

Harriet was speechless. Was that really what she'd said?

"Some have come here simply to see Dr. Harold Bailey's collection of paintings, propelled no doubt by their own love of animals. Others have come and asked what they can do to help in the search for Nessie. But several have come with a very different goal in mind."

Harriet braced herself.

Candace pinned her with a probing gaze. "Sources tell me you've received several offers for your grandfather's painting since YTV first reported Nessie's abduction."

"We always have offers," Harriet said evenly.

"Yes, but have they been as high as twenty-two thousand pounds before? Who knew a stolen cat could be so lucrative?"

CHAPTER EIGHT

Harriet tucked the edges of her warmest blanket around her waist and settled into the sofa's comfy cushions with a bowl of freshly popped popcorn. It had been a long day, made longer by an unexpected late-day surgery on a beagle who'd swallowed a small ball. But now, with the beagle recovering and the boarders having been cared for, she could finally stop and breathe.

Charlie jumped up beside her, and Harriet scratched between the feline's ears. "I didn't see much of you today, sweet girl. How was your day?"

She smiled down at the squeak-free dog parked beside her feet. "Those of us who chose to stay in the clinic certainly had our share of excitement. Didn't we, Maxwell?"

The dog leaned against her leg and gazed up at her in pure adoration.

Harriet grabbed the remote control from the coffee table and aimed it at the television. "The evening news should be starting in a few minutes. And we're going to hope I'm not on it. Here we go."

A man in his fifties appeared on the screen in a gray suit. "Good evening, everyone. I'm Giles Cooke with YTV."

He proceeded to walk listeners through the day in Yorkshire, England, and the world as a whole. No mention of Harriet or the missing cat.

Harriet was about to breathe a sigh of relief and shut off the TV when her hopes were dashed.

"And finally, YTV has been flooded with inquiries about Nessie, the cat missing from White Church Bay, as reported by our own Candace Moore on Sunday. For an update on Nessie, let's go to Candace live in the field."

Harriet groaned.

Standing beneath an umbrella, Candace's welcoming smile quickly gave way to a serious demeanor. "Good evening. I'm standing outside Cobble Hill Farm, the property once owned by the late Dr. Harold Bailey, a beloved White Church Bay veterinarian."

"You're still here?" Harriet demanded as her phone rang. She scooped it up and answered. "Hello?"

"Are you watching the news?" Aunt Jinny asked. "Candace Moore is reporting from here."

"I know. I heard her say that too."

"I can see her right this very minute," Aunt Jinny said. "Or at least I can see the top of her brolly—sorry, her umbrella—from my kitchen window."

Harriet watched the recording playing out on the screen in front of her while Candace continued to speak—the clinic's parking area, the line of people waiting outside the gallery, inquisitive faces studying the painting of Nessie inside the gallery, and—

"That's you, Harriet!" Aunt Jinny exclaimed.

Harriet stared at the shot of herself standing in the middle of the waiting room. She took in her pale pink vet coat, faded jeans, her unkempt hair and the way it seemed to escape her ponytail holder on all sides, and the discomfort plain on her face.

"Who knew a stolen cat could be so lucrative?" Candace said on screen.

Aunt Jinny's gasp echoed in Harriet's ear as Harriet's dumbstruck expression was replaced on the screen by Candace standing beneath her umbrella against a night sky. "Who took Nessie and why? That's what everyone here in White Church Bay and across the entire YTV viewing area is asking themselves tonight. But perhaps there's another, more sinister question we should all be asking. Who stands to gain the most from the abduction of this sweet, seven-toed feline? Back to you, Giles."

Harriet sank onto the couch with a long exhale and shut off the television. "I'm so glad that's over."

"Well, I never," Aunt Jinny seethed. "She's making it sound like you orchestrated Nessie's disappearance for financial gain!"

Dropping her head back against the couch, Harriet closed her eyes. "No, Candace Moore knows people could offer a lot more than they have and we'd still never sell that painting."

"How does she know that?"

"Because I told her."

"They didn't show you saying that."

"Thank goodness they cut it." Harriet's laugh sounded tired even to her own ears. "I looked and sounded so unprofessional."

"But their editing made it sound like you kidnapped Nessie to sell the painting."

Harriet jack-knifed upright on the couch. "You don't think people will think that, do you? Aunt Jinny, I don't care if someone handed me a million pounds for that painting. It's not for sale."

"I know that, Harriet, but I've known you since you were a baby. I'm not everyone, and there's no denying the sudden, intense interest in Nessie's painting since Candace Moore did that first story on Sunday night."

"The pictures they showed of the line to get into the gallery today didn't do it justice," Harriet murmured.

"And how did she know the amount of that offer?"

"I don't know. It was in a sealed envelope when I got it. I still have the offers themselves because I want you to see them, but I didn't think they were anywhere she'd have access to."

"We'll have to figure that out," Aunt Jinny said.

Harriet sighed. "Now the hordes of animal lovers won't line up outside the gallery to see Grandad's painting. They'll be lining up outside the clinic to string me up by my toes for stealing Nessie."

"You didn't steal Nessie."

"You know that and I know that. And Polly knows it, if for no other reason than she thinks Tarquin wanted Nessie out of the way in order to get a dog he's already named. But that news show reaches a lot of people, and they didn't get to hear me answer Candace's question."

"Then call the station first thing tomorrow and demand that people do," Aunt Jinny said firmly. "Either by the station airing your answer or retracting a question that came across as an insinuation."

Harriet gazed at the peaceful grounds and wondered how much longer that peace would last. "Van really needs to find Nessie, Aunt Jinny. For Cindy, and now for me."

Harriet settled Murphy in his kennel and Princess in the new roaming pen then promised to return at lunch to check on them.

"That pen is big enough for both of them at the same time."

Harriet glanced over her shoulder and smiled at Mike. "It would be if they got along while they're unsupervised, but they don't. Princess isn't crazy about Murphy, though he'd love to be friends if she'd allow it."

"You're good with animals."

Harriet laughed. "I'd hope so, since they're my livelihood."

"Did you spend a lot of time here when you were growing up?" Mike asked. "You know, watching your grandfather take care of animals?"

"Not as much as I would've liked, but I soaked up everything I could when I got to visit."

"Is your grandfather why you became a veterinarian?"

"He is. I thought he had the coolest job, in the coolest place."

"And now?"

"Now, thanks to him in more ways than one, I have the coolest job in the coolest place."

The handyman ran his hand along the top of the chest-high pen he'd built. "It's a beautiful home. I can't imagine having so much space." Mike dropped his hand back to his side. "My flat isn't much bigger than this pen. And before you hired me, I wasn't sure I could even keep that. But I'm a little less worried now."

"I'm glad to hear it. You've made some amazing improvements around here, and I'm grateful. For example, this pen is even better than what I was picturing in my head. You've set it up so they have more room than I hoped for. It will be really nice for my high-energy boarders."

"I'm glad you like it." He cleared his throat. "Did you happen to watch the news last night?"

Harriet blew out a breath. "If you're referring to the segment on Nessie and the painting, yes, I did. Unfortunately. And I know how it sounded too." After she'd hung up with Aunt Jinny, her cousin Anthony, Polly, and Doreen Danby had all called to check in with her as well.

"I called the station last night," Mike said, trailing her out of the barn.

Harriet spun to face him. "You did? Why?"

"To tell them they had no right cutting out your response," Mike said. "That it left an impression that wasn't accurate or fair."

"Thank you, Mike. I really appreciate it."

"I really appreciate this job and you for giving it to me." He glanced at his watch. "Which means I should probably start working on the loose doorjamb from my to-do list."

"And I better get myself into the clinic before Polly sends out the search party. We're due to open in five minutes."

"I'll let you get to it then." He started down the garden path toward the gallery's back door. "Have a brilliant day, Doc."

He was barely out of sight when the sound of him bellowing her name shattered the morning quiet.

She sprinted for the gallery.

But when she rounded the corner, Mike held out his hand. "Hang on. Don't touch anything."

She halted in her tracks and saw that one of the gallery windows was broken. "What on earth happened here? I know it was windy last night, but not enough to break a window, right?"

Mike peered through the gap where the glass had been. "You better call the police."

"Why? What's wrong?"

"The wind didn't break this window. That chair from the patio did. And your grandfather's painting of Nessie is gone."

Harriet stood in the corner behind Ida's desk and did her best to process the scene in front of her. A tall, dark-haired male officer dusted for prints. A shorter, blond female officer inspected the door the thief had clearly used to exit the gallery with Grandad's painting. Van sealed the note they'd found into an evidence bag.

From where she stood, she couldn't read the block letters on the sheet of paper. But it didn't matter. They'd burned themselves into her mind's eye when she'd seen them where the painting of Nessie should have been.

NOW YOU KNOW WHAT IT'S LIKE.

"You okay, Harriet?" Van asked gently.

"Not really. I don't understand why someone would do this."

"Nessie's painting has gotten a lot of attention these past few days," Van said.

"Sure, but it's still just a painting. It doesn't mean anything to anyone but me."

"It's a painting people are willing to pay for, according to last night's news." Van handed the evidence bag to another officer then pulled a notebook and pen from his pocket. "Which we need to talk about."

Harriet rubbed the ache forming at her left temple. "We've always gotten offers for that painting, Van. People love it. They love everything from the story itself to the huge paws on a tiny kitten."

"But now that Nessie is missing, you've gotten higher offers, correct?"

"Yes."

"How much were they for?"

"One was for twenty thousand, the other twenty-two thousand," she said.

Van gaped at her. "Seriously?"

She nodded.

"Wow," he murmured as he made notes. "How much have you been offered in the past?"

"Nowhere near that. Ida will have the exact numbers."

"Do we know the names of the people who made those large offers?" Van asked. "And did they say those numbers out loud, to your knowledge?"

"I don't believe so. Each handed Ida an envelope with the offer inside. Both envelopes included a written offer and contact information."

"Do you still have the offers?"

"I do. I wanted Aunt Jinny to see them, though I'm going to refuse them. Would you like to see them?"

Van returned the notebook and pen to his pocket. "That would be grand."

She led the way out of the gallery. "I could use the change of scenery."

But when she reached the living room, she stopped so suddenly that Van nearly ran into her.

The end table where she'd left the offers was bare.

CHAPTER NINE

"M aybe you threw them away and don't remember it," Polly suggested.

Harriet glanced across the outdoor bench at her receptionist and friend. "I thought about it. I even balled them up. But then I decided I should show them to Aunt Jinny and left them on the table next to the couch."

"We'll find them, Harriet," Polly assured her.

"But you helped me scour the entire living room just now. And we even dug through the trash can I know I didn't put them into."

"We did, but we can look again," Polly said. "After we take a little time out here to breathe. And Van will find the painting. I know he will." She peered toward the parking lot. "Now that's interesting."

"What is?" Harriet followed Polly's gaze and groaned at the sight of Candace Moore and her cameraman, Doug, exiting their van in the parking area.

Dressed in a pair of black trousers and a rose-colored blouse, Candace joined them. "You must be devastated, Ms. Bailey."

"*Dr.* Bailey," Polly corrected sharply.

"We heard about the break-in at your grandfather's gallery and the theft of the painting you said you'd never sell." Candace nodded to Doug and then turned back to Harriet. "So I repeat, you must be devastated."

Harriet exchanged a glance with Polly then cleared her throat. "I *am* devastated. That painting was a link to my late grandfather, a man I cherished and admired. Every day I try to be as great a veterinarian and person of integrity as he was. That painting was one my family and I would never have sold, though no one would know it from your last segment. Some things in life are simply worth more than money."

Candace faced the camera. "While the Bailey family mourns the loss of their beloved painting, one can't help but wonder if the disappearances of Nessie and her painting are connected. And if so, how?"

After a few seconds of silence counted down with his fingers, Doug lowered the camera from his shoulder. "Nice work, Candace. Do you want to be there when I document the thief's entry point, or do you want me to meet you back here when I'm done?"

"The latter is fine." Candace claimed the empty spot on the bench between Harriet and Polly. "Phew. You have no idea how good it feels to sit down. I've literally been on my feet since I left my flat this morning."

Harriet held her tongue.

"Even with a note making it clear Nessie was taken rather than just missing, my colleagues thought I shouldn't do this story," Candace said in a confidential tone. "'It's a cat,' they said. 'Who cares?' But I knew I could make it into something. Now that the painting is missing, those same colleagues are starting to look at me differently."

Harriet clenched her jaw so hard she was afraid her teeth might crack. A woman was in torment over her missing pet, she herself mourned a lost connection with her late grandfather, and this reporter was gloating over a successful story?

"More importantly, though, the higher-ups are looking at me differently." Candace plucked a piece of fuzz from her trousers then froze, her eyes wide. "Can we forget I said that out loud? I don't want to jinx myself. In fact, I probably should get back to work before Doug gets antsy."

The reporter hurried toward the gallery and disappeared around the corner.

"Well, that was interesting," Polly murmured.

"Wasn't it though?" Harriet checked her phone to find a text message from Van. "The new note matches the first one we got—same lettering, same kind of paper."

"So whoever took Nessie probably took the painting as well," Polly said. "Tarquin could steal a painting."

"I suppose he could. But why would he leave a note that says, 'Now you know what it's like'?"

"To throw us off?" Polly suggested.

Harriet made a face. "That's a stretch. I think it's safe to say that I'm the 'you' referred to in the note."

Polly leaned forward. "Not necessarily. The you could be Cindy. Tarquin wanted a dog, but she said no. Now she doesn't have Nessie."

"I don't see it, but we'll leave him as a possibility—a remote possibility." Harriet got up and began to pace. "Do we have any more likely suspects?"

"Maybe someone whose ultimate goal was Doc Bailey's painting from the start?" Polly suggested. "And they thought taking Nessie first would increase its value. They were right, based on those offers you got."

"And lost."

"They'll turn up, I'm sure. Just like Nessie and the painting." Polly stood. "If you're correct, and the note was aimed at you, what feeling might losing the painting have given you?"

"What it's like to have something important to me taken?" Harriet mused. "I can't think of anything else."

"Well, whoever it is, they're obviously harboring some kind of anger toward you."

That reminded her of something. "Dale Renner is angry with me over my diagnosis of Scout."

"But you weren't responsible. I sent him the report like you asked, so he should know that."

"If he reads the report and believes it."

Polly folded her arms over her chest. "Maybe he stole the painting, but why would he take a cat that doesn't belong to you?"

"For the reason you suggested," Harriet said. "To drive up the price of the painting. Perhaps he intends to sell it to help pay for Scout's new food. In the States, people occasionally sue for emotional distress. I wonder if he thought he wouldn't win such a case here, so he decided to take matters into his own hands."

"I suppose that could make sense. Should we loop Van in on this?"

Harriet considered the option. "I don't want to subject Mr. Renner to something as unsettling as a police interrogation when we don't have any evidence. I'd rather wait and see if we can find anything out ourselves."

"And you think he's going to talk to you?"

"I have to try."

Polly pointed at a car as it entered the parking area. "Get some rest, boss. With all the appointments we had to reschedule today, tomorrow is going to be packed."

"I will. And you too." Harriet watched Polly hurry over to her car and then waved when her friend glanced back. "Thanks for everything today."

Polly waved, and drove away.

Aunt Jinny hurried around the corner of the house. "Harriet, are you okay? Have you gotten any word on the painting? I'm so sorry I couldn't get away from work until now."

Harriet stood and stepped into her aunt's waiting arms, the warm embrace a much-needed comfort. "I'm so sorry I didn't hear the window shattering last night or early this morning."

Aunt Jinny grabbed hold of Harriet's shoulders, her dark blue eyes round with surprise. "I'm glad you didn't, dear. If you had, you might've gone outside, and there's no telling what might have happened."

"But Grandad's gallery." Harriet's breath hitched. "His painting."

Aunt Jinny peered into her eyes. "You were more important to your grandad than either of those things, Harriet. Always."

Harriet sank back onto the bench. "I just ache at the thought of never seeing that painting again. Because it's *him*. In many ways that painting is Grandad. It shows so much of his views and beliefs, like Nessie holding on to hope in spite of a situation that was clearly terrifying for her."

"Did you get that?"

Harriet twisted on the bench to find Candace standing behind Doug, who nodded and lowered his camera to his side.

Aunt Jinny stormed over to the reporter. "I called your station to lodge a complaint about you and your disgusting editing of my niece. You have some nerve coming back here."

Harriet hurried to catch up with her aunt. "Aunt Jinny, it's okay. I knew they were here. They were over at the gallery, getting shots of the broken window."

"For what reason?" Aunt Jinny demanded of Candace.

"Whether we like it or not, Aunt Jinny, the break-in at Grandad's gallery is news."

Candace beamed at them. "That exchange on the bench was absolute gold."

The cameraman looked at his watch. "We should probably get into position for when we go live."

Candace tapped her chin with her finger. "Yesterday we were out by the Cobble Hill Farm sign. Today let's shoot by the gallery door."

"I'll get set up while you finish here." Doug walked away.

Aunt Jinny eyed Candace sharply. "If you take the kind of liberties with this segment that you took with last night's, you will not be permitted on this property ever again. Are we clear?"

Candace made no reply, but her bright smile held a fierce quality that put Harriet on edge.

CHAPTER TEN

arriet had just put a kettle of water on the stove when a quiet knock from the other end of the hall caught her by surprise.

She sighed. She had really been looking forward to the day being over.

She followed Charlie and Maxwell toward the front door and the shadowy figure she could make out through the sidelight. Her thoughts skittered to the break-in that had started her day, and she found her steps slowing. After all, darkness was encroaching, and she hadn't invited anyone over.

Another knock, this one a bit louder, was followed by a muffled yet familiar voice from the other side of the door. "Harriet? Are you home? I know it would've been more proper to call first, but—"

She opened the door to the handsome man on her doorstep holding a small white bag.

"Will? Is—is everything okay?"

"I'm here to ask you that. I heard about the break-in."

Harriet waved him inside. "Please come in."

"I don't mean to intrude on your evening." He entered and offered her the white bag. "Doreen Danby brought biscuits to Bible study this afternoon, and I thought you might be in need of a treat after everything that's happened."

"I might be. Especially if you'll have hot chocolate with me."

"Are you sure?" he asked. "You were probably hoping to decompress, not play hostess."

"Quite sure. Maxwell and Charlie will appreciate a break in my aimless pacing."

Will crouched to greet the animals. "Hello, Maxwell, Charlie." He smiled up at Harriet. "I was with Harold when we came across Charlie in that burning bin. It's wonderful to see her so healthy and happy." He gave Charlie one last scratch and stood. "Like Nessie was with Cindy Summerton until someone stole her."

Harriet slumped against the wall. "I don't understand any of what's going on, Will—from Nessie being stolen from her home to her painting being stolen from the gallery without my hearing a sound." Shaking her head, she motioned for him to follow her into the kitchen. "Come on. I'll get us that hot chocolate I mentioned. It'll go well with the cookies."

When they were settled at the kitchen table with steaming mugs of cocoa, Will leaned forward. "Do the police have any leads on who could have taken the painting?"

Harriet wrapped her hands around the warm mug. "Not yet, unfortunately."

"I'm sorry to hear that."

She sipped her cocoa. "This past weekend, Charlie led me to a box of tapes my grandad recorded. One of them explains how he was inspired to start painting, and the others tell the stories of some of the animals he chose as his subjects. I haven't had time to listen to them all, but the ones I have heard are wonderful. To hear his voice, to hear him talk about the animals he painted and why they spoke to him the way they did—it's been such a treat. Almost a chance to visit with him again, if only for a little while."

Will took and briefly squeezed her hand. "Your grandfather would be proud of you, Harriet. I'm sure of it."

"For what?" she asked bitterly. "For losing his favorite painting?"

"First and foremost, you are not responsible for that break-in." Will's tone was adamant. "But I'm talking about him being proud of how you're continuing his work here—caring for everyone's animals. I know many of the locals resisted you at first, but I also know you're winning them over."

She raised an eyebrow. "Have you looked me up online in the past few days? I have two one-star ratings, and the clinic has one as well."

Surprise marched across his face. "They must be a mistake."

Her answering laugh was void of humor. "They're not. They're from Dale Renner."

"He can't blame you for his dog's food allergies."

"He does. He still thinks I'm lying to make him pay me more. Fortunately, I've had three new patients this past week, so I guess online reviews aren't everything. And I have two boarders in the barn right now. One staying until Friday, the other until Saturday."

"I thought I heard someone barking when I pulled up." Will glanced down at the table, fiddled with the spoon she'd set beside his mug, and, finally, lifted his gaze back to Harriet's. "I'm guessing there's still been no word on Nessie either?"

She grimaced. "None."

"How awful. And I heard you've been receiving offers for the painting of her."

78

"We've always gotten offers for that painting, but they've been much higher since the news broke about the subject being stolen. Polly has suggested that someone stole Nessie to drive up the painting's value."

"Unfortunately, that theory isn't impossible."

Before she could respond, her phone rang, and she stood reluctantly. "I should probably check who that is in case it's the police or a vet emergency."

"No worries." He rose as well. "I should be heading out anyway. Thank you for the cocoa and the hospitality. It made for a very nice evening."

She checked her screen. "It's Polly. I can call her back."

"Talk to her, Harriet. Friends are important during difficult times."

"You're right. They are. Thank you for being one tonight, Will."

He smiled. "Of course. It was my pleasure. And don't forget that I'm only a phone call away if you need anything." And then he was gone.

She connected the call right before it would have gone to voice mail. "Hi, Polly. Is everything okay?"

"The clinic phone has been ringing off the hook since tonight's story on the telly."

"When? I haven't heard it at all."

"That's because I forwarded the calls to my phone before I left," Polly said, her words periodically broken by an odd *thump* followed by groans. "I figured you'd had enough today."

"Thank you, Polly, but you shouldn't have to work at—"

Thump.

"What is that sound?" Harriet asked.

"I'm at the Crow's Nest, scoring a round of darts. You're hearing the opposing team's turn, specifically this guy, Theo, who claimed he could play darts but clearly can't."

Harriet laughed. "I imagine Van is thrilled."

"If he were here, he would be. Instead, Mike is thrilled."

"*Our* Mike?"

"One and the same."

Harriet stepped into the living room and sank onto the couch. "Are you on a date?"

Polly laughed. "No. Put your mind at ease. Van had to bail on account of a certain break-in he's working. Mike was here and stepped into his spot. But guess who else is here?"

"Who?"

"Candace Moore and her cameraman."

"Why?"

"To grab some dinner after her report, I guess. Or, at least, Doug is. Candace is enjoying the attention. Just about everyone in here was glued to the telly mere minutes before she and Doug showed up. I recognized where Candace was standing, and I wanted to make sure she didn't hang you out to dry again."

"She didn't."

"I saw that. Which is good, because I think your aunt would've put on battle armor otherwise."

Harriet recalled Aunt Jinny's firm words to the reporter. "You're not wrong."

"That said, people are talking about you pretty much everywhere in this place right now."

"You mean the break-in, right?"

"No, I mean *you*."

"Why?"

"Your grandfather was well loved in this village. Some folks might not have been too sure about you coming in and taking over for him, but they were willing to give you a chance because you're his kin. You're winning over our current clients with the quality of your work and care. But when Doug caught you and Jinny talking about how much you miss Doc Bailey, the atmosphere changed in here. If we get calls from half the people I've heard talking about you tonight, we'll be booked solid at the clinic for weeks."

"But that's not why I said that stuff to Aunt Jinny."

"Of course not," Polly said. "It was quite clear you didn't even know Doug and Candace were there. If that segment gets some new patients in the door, your skill and your experience with the animals will keep them coming back."

"I guess, but—"

"Lest I inflate your ego too much, your bench chat didn't have the same effect on everyone here. A couple people chose to see something different than everyone else saw. Or, at least, Dale Renner did. I saw him and Theo talking to Doug a few minutes ago."

"Wait." Harriet tightened her hold on the phone. "Dale Renner?"

"Yes. He's Theo's darts partner tonight, poor guy."

"Did you talk to Dale?" Harriet asked.

"I tried to. I asked him how he was doing. I complimented him on a few of his throws. I asked if he likes cats. But he's having none of it. He won't talk to me."

"You asked him if he likes cats?" Harriet asked.

"Sure. I was trying to feel out whether he might have taken Nessie."

"Subtle, Polly. Does Theo agree with Dale about what happened to Scout?"

"I think Theo's an awkward guy who came to the Crow's Nest because he had nothing else to do. He's filling in for Max's no-show darts partner, and he's trying not to rock the boat. I wouldn't lose any sleep over it if I were you."

"But you said they were talking to Doug," Harriet fretted. "Doug, who's already helped Candace with a rather skewed portrayal of me."

"If by some miracle Candace hasn't already seen Dale's reviews online, she was going to find them eventually. With or without Dale's help."

"Am I supposed to feel comfort in that?"

"I was thinking more you could use that information to prepare yourself in case it comes up in another interview with Candace," Polly replied. "And before I forget, Theresa Wallace was one of the calls I fielded."

"Is everything okay with her parrot?"

"I don't know, but she asked for you to return her call. Tonight, if you can."

"I'll call her right now," Harriet said. "Anything else?"

"Nothing that can't wait. And my team is up again, so I've got to go. See you in the morning, okay?"

"Thank you, Polly," Harriet said. "For always having my back. For keeping things running smoothly at the clinic. And for being my friend. You're quite a blessing in my life."

"Same to ya."

Harriet grinned. "I hope you and Mike get your win."

"Oh, I'm pretty sure we got it the moment Theo started playing." Polly's voice grew serious again. "And Harriet?"

"Yes?"

"Make sure the doors are all locked before you call it a night, okay?"

CHAPTER ELEVEN

Theresa Wallace picked up on the first ring, her voice full of worry. "Hello?"

"Theresa, this is Harriet—"

"Oh, thank you so much for calling back. I was afraid you wouldn't get the message until morning."

"My assistant prioritizes well." After flipping the light switch inside the study, Harriet made a beeline for the veterinary books that filled Grandad's shelves. "Tell me what's going on with Wilson."

"All these new sounds he's making are driving me batty."

In the background, Harriet could hear the squeak of Wilson's cage door opening. "Tell me about them."

"For example, I got out of bed much earlier than usual this morning because it sounded like someone was bumping around inside the cottage. I grabbed the baseball bat I keep under my bed and searched the place, but there was nothing, and nothing had fallen. But as I was heading back into my bedroom, I heard it again. And I realized it was coming from Wilson."

Harriet grabbed the book she wanted and skimmed a section on African grays. "So what kind of call was it?"

"This wasn't a call," Theresa said. "I'm familiar with most of his calls, but lately he's been doing sound effects. After the thumps, he made another sound like nails on a chalkboard. It made me want to scream. But as I was trying to get him to stop, he made this pathetic little whimper, which he's been doing a lot lately, and then went totally silent."

Harriet carried the open book to her desk and sat down, mulling over Theresa's words. "Has he continued plucking his feathers?"

"He's been messing with them off and on since I brought him in to see you, but he didn't actually pluck another one out until tonight."

"And what was happening when he did that?" Harriet asked.

"I was watching the news on the break-in at your gallery and the ongoing search for that woman's cat."

"Interesting."

A soft meow from somewhere in the distance made Harriet abandon her grandfather's book and head off in search of Charlie.

"Is there any chance you could take a look at Wilson again tomorrow?" Theresa asked. "Just to be sure there's nothing else going on?"

Squatting down, Harriet scratched behind Maxwell's ears while peering into the kitchen and living room. Another soft, distant meow met her ears, and she straightened to follow it. "Yes, I can fit Wilson in tomorrow. Can you bring him in around noon?" That was usually her lunch break, but at least she knew she wouldn't have any other appointments at that time.

"We'll be there. Thank you."

"If anything comes up between now and then, call me at this number. It's my personal cell, and I'll have it next to my bed tonight."

"You don't have to do that. You barely even know me."

"I can see how much you care about Wilson. That's enough for me."

"Thank you," Theresa whispered. "I just came back into the room, and he's got his head tucked down."

"Everything you're saying makes me think he's afraid of something," Harriet mused. "Did you bring anything new into the house either today or yesterday by any chance? Something he might find threatening?"

"No. I haven't left this place in the last two days," Theresa replied. "The glamorous life of a best-selling novelist, right? Anyway, I should let you go. Thank you for returning my call, and thank you for agreeing to see Wilson tomorrow."

Harriet squinted at the couch, one end obscured by a throw pillow out of place. "Of course. We'll do our best to get Wilson back to his old self again. Sooner rather than later."

With the call over, Harriet lowered the phone and listened for a meow or any other indication that Charlie was in trouble. Instead, all she heard was a quiet, steady purr.

She crept toward the couch, the soft purr growing louder with each step, then gently lifted the pillow.

Wound in a tight ball and pressed between the back of the couch and the throw pillow was Charlie, her white-tipped paws covering her face. She purred steadily in her sleep.

Harriet breathed a sigh of relief. At least one animal in her care wasn't in crisis.

Harriet had tried all the usual tricks, interspersed with a few of her own, to fall asleep.

She'd counted sheep, then dogs. She'd willed herself to focus on the rise and fall of her breath. She'd downed a mug of warm milk. She'd read a chapter of a book she wasn't loving. She'd listened to her grandfather's voice talking about the moment he'd first laid eyes on Nessie.

She'd built a pen for the sheep in her thoughts, realized she could elongate her exhales for an impressively long time, discovered that Charlie and Maxwell liked to sleep in a pile together in the living room, abandoned the book, and vowed to move heaven and earth to find both Grandad's beloved painting and Nessie—if only so she could sleep again someday.

When the first hint of daylight reached through her window, Harriet slid her feet over the edge of the bed and into her waiting slippers. She knew it wasn't good to be going into a full day on a few hours of substandard sleep, but knowing it and fixing it were two very different things.

After getting dressed, Harriet pulled her dark brown hair into a ponytail and secured it with the scrunchie she'd left on the nightstand.

"First things first," she told herself. "Strong coffee."

The stairs creaked under her feet as she made her way down to the first floor. She flicked on the kitchen light to find Charlie dropping a piece of dog food in front of Maxwell, who gobbled it up.

"Does she do this for you every morning, buddy?" Harriet asked.

Maxwell yipped as if in confirmation. He slept without his wheels at night, so it was hard for him to make it to his food bowl. The fact that Charlie had decided to help him touched Harriet.

Squatting down, she ran her hand along Charlie's back and tail. "You're quite the little actress, aren't you? All this time you've pretended to be completely ambivalent toward Maxwell, but you do actually care about him, don't you?"

Charlie's tail flicked Harriet's nose in response, and Harriet smiled as she attached Maxwell's prosthesis. "There you go, Maxwell. It's off to the races for you now too."

He scampered to his water bowl for a drink, finished up his kibble, and returned to Harriet for an ear scratch.

"I'm sorry we're up so early today, but I tried. I really did." Harriet finished petting the animals and stood. "So, what do you think, you two? Coffee first? Or take the boarders out for their preclinic walk?"

She thought about Murphy, who'd be reunited with his beloved owner in a little over twenty-four hours. She'd miss the sweet dog, but she was glad he would be where he belonged.

"Okay, it's settled. I'll take them on a walk, then have coffee." Harriet crossed to the coatrack, plucked her hooded rain jacket off its hook, and shrugged into it with a loud yawn.

Once outside, she shivered in the crisp morning air and zipped her jacket all the way to her chin. The part of her that despised cold and damp urged her to walk quickly, but she slowed her steps, inhaled the moist air, and watched her exhales appear as white plumes around her face. She was determined to start her day on the best possible note.

Even in the early light of day, she could feel her grandfather in this place—his presence, his importance in her life, her determined commitment to make him proud.

"One day at a time," she said, even as her thoughts recounted to the obstacles that had risen in front of her in just the last few days.

Yet as Grandad always said, there were good things to be found among the bad. And he was right. Inside the same week that had brought so much turmoil, she'd welcomed several new patients, filled next week's schedule, gotten a surprise visit from Will that had filled her heart in a way she'd yet to decipher, seen her idea for a new pen inside the barn come to fruition, and—

A loud bark made her laugh.

"And yes, Murphy, I've had the pleasure of some nice walks with you and Princess."

A second, louder bark from the Labrador drowned out the sound of the latch she disengaged on the green wooden gate that stood between her and the barn. "I'm coming, boy."

She listened for Princess to have her say too, but there was nothing.

"Too much of a lady to holler at me, Princess?" Harriet chuckled as she pulled the door open.

But only Murphy barked.

Unease creeping up her spine, Harriet hurried inside then froze at the sight that greeted her.

"Princess?"

Goose bumps broke over her skin as her stomach fell to her feet.

The poodle's cage was empty.

Murphy's bark grew louder, more insistent as Harriet scrubbed her hands down the sides of her face. She hadn't slept well, but she remembered securing Princess's cage, then Murphy's before bed last night. Except Murphy was where he belonged, and Princess was not.

Harriet ran around the pen to the far side of the barn and the pair of empty stables she'd yet to convert into kennels. Nothing.

She turned back to the open barn door and stared out at her grandfather's garden, her mind's eye picturing Princess making a break for her owner's home. The poodle was smart—there was no doubt about that. But even Princess couldn't unlatch a cage or open and close a barn door that had a handle she couldn't reach.

Harriet dashed out of the barn right into Mike, whose tools on his belt rattled against one another.

"Whoa! What's the rush?" he asked.

"Someone took Princess," she told him. "I have to call the police, and my phone is in the house."

Mike reached into his jeans pocket, pulled out a phone, and handed it to Harriet. "Use mine. I'll search the grounds. We'll find her."

"Why would someone take her?" she asked him. "I don't understand."

"I don't either. But we'll get her back."

CHAPTER TWELVE

H arriet? How did she take it?"

Harriet lifted her head from her hands. "Not well, Polly."

Polly came into the office and perched on Harriet's desk. "What did Miss Greer say?"

Harriet massaged her temples, the woman's irate tone ringing in her ears. "She cried as she talked about getting Princess as a puppy, how Princess has been her one true companion in life, and that she picked me to care for Princess during her first holiday in ten years because I was Harold's granddaughter, so I must be competent."

Polly rested a hand on Harriet's shoulder. "How awful."

"Then she told me I'm nothing like Grandad because he would never have let something like this happen if Princess had been boarded with him." Harriet ran a hand down her face. "And she's totally right."

"No, she's upset and lashing out from shock," Polly said. "She'll come around."

Harriet blew out a frustrated breath. "She *should* be upset. I lost her dog."

"You didn't lose her, Harriet. She was stolen, which is entirely the fault of the thief, not you. Those are two very different things. We've never lost a boarder."

"It's the same result."

"Everyone is searching for her, including those who came in for appointments."

Harriet snorted. "You mean those who came in for an appointment and left the second they heard why there were police everywhere?"

"I think they were just being respectful of the stress you're under," Polly answered calmly.

"Right." Harriet pushed back from her desk and stood. "And how many of the ones who left made another appointment?"

Polly bit her lip, her silence all the answer Harriet needed.

"I can't blame them. Can you?" Harriet stepped around Polly and wandered over to the window. "I mean, would you entrust the well-being of your pet to a woman who allowed someone's dog to be stolen on her watch?"

The desk creaked as Polly joined Harriet at the window. "You didn't *allow* Princess to be stolen, Harriet."

"She was in my care. In my barn."

"As was Murphy, and he's still here," Polly pointed out.

Harriet spun around. "I never walked him."

"I did while you were on the phone with Miss Greer."

"Telling her that her dog is gone," Harriet murmured.

Polly laid a hand on her shoulder. "I know this is hard and awful. I know that telling Miss Greer about Princess was difficult. But we will find her. I'm sure of it. In the meantime, I think you need to check on Murphy yourself."

A chill ran down Harriet's spine. "Why? Is something wrong with him?"

"No. I think he's stressed by all the new faces in and out of the barn this morning. He seemed to enjoy our walk, but it seemed to me he was searching for you the whole time."

"I should have thought of that. Of course he's stressed. Not only because of the police being around but because he would've seen Princess get taken."

"If only he could talk," Polly mused.

"If only." Harriet squeezed Polly's hand. "Thank you for handling everything I couldn't this morning. I was really upset, but you've gotten my head back on straight, and now I'm ready to face things."

Polly gave her a bright smile. "That's what friends are for—helping us keep hope and perspective. We'll find Princess."

"I pray you're right. In the meantime, I'm going to check on Murphy."

Footsteps sounded in the lobby followed by the sound of a woman's voice calling, "Hello? Is anyone here?"

"I don't have any appointments scheduled until after lunch," Polly whispered.

"Not that they'll actually let me touch their pets once they find out what happened," Harriet said.

Rolling her eyes, Polly shoved past Harriet and stepped into the reception area. "Hello, Ms. Wallace. And hello to you too, Wilson. I'm sorry, but I don't have you scheduled for an appointment today."

Harriet smacked herself in the forehead as she hurried out front. In the morning's chaos, she'd completely forgotten about the informal appointment she'd made with Theresa the night before. "I knew they were coming, Polly. Hi, Theresa. No change since we last spoke?"

Theresa shook her head, her lower lip trembling. "Actually, he plucked another feather from the same spot as last time during the night. And he made a new sound this morning, over and over again."

"Poor little guy. You're really going through something right now, aren't you, Wilson?" Harriet murmured to the parrot. She beckoned to Theresa. "Bring him into an exam room so I can take a closer look."

"Thank you, Harriet."

As she passed Polly's desk, Harriet said, "By the way, I believe Mike has an eye on Murphy while he's adding a dead bolt to the barn door, but I'd feel a lot better if Murphy was in here with us."

"I'll go get him."

"Thanks, Polly."

Harriet squared her shoulders and stepped into the exam room with Theresa and Wilson. She carefully washed her hands and braced herself for the potential results of full disclosure then said, "Before we go any further, I think it's only fair to tell you why the police are here."

"Because of the stolen dog, right?"

Harriet drew back. "You know?"

"I saw it on the news as I was leaving to come here," Theresa said.

"And you still came?" Harriet blurted out before she could think better of it.

"Of course I did. Why wouldn't I? You didn't ask to be attacked from all angles at the same time like this. I was worried you wouldn't have time to see Wilson in the midst of all of it, but I never questioned whether I wanted you to."

94

"I'm glad to hear that." Harriet gently extracted the parrot from the cage to examine him. "So why are you plucking your feathers, sweet boy? What's got you so upset?"

Theresa's face was pinched with worry. "I took your advice after the last visit and did my best to stay with him as much as possible. I've even had my groceries delivered. I got my daily dose of fresh air by sitting in a chair he could see from the screened-in porch. And I made a point of playing my favorite songs when I wasn't writing in hopes they would give him a sense of familiarity."

"Good, good," Harriet murmured, managing not to yelp when the bird bit her hand.

"Wilson," Theresa scolded him. "That's not very nice. I'm so sorry, Harriet."

"He's stressed and afraid. This isn't the first time I've been bitten, and it won't be the last," Harriet assured her. "Don't worry about it." When Wilson released her finger, she moved it about in the air, watching how he tracked her movement. Rotating him slowly, she studied the section he'd plucked free of feathers.

"I thought maybe he was getting used to things, because he didn't pluck again for a while after that first time." Theresa made soft kissing sounds at Wilson as Harriet moved him this way and that then said, "And he only made his crazy new sounds when I woke up in the morning."

"Maybe he decided to change his greeting since you changed his world?" Harriet teased. "His version of getting even, perhaps?"

Theresa managed a smile despite her obvious worry. "It sure seems that way. But this morning, he kicked it off with a brand-new sound several times in a row. When he was done with that, he moved to the same litany of sounds he's been making since Saturday, adding the new one at the end."

"Can you imitate it?"

"I can try. But you might want to cover your ears. It's rather shrill."

Harriet placed Wilson back in his cage, shut the door, and covered her ears. "Go ahead." She carefully watched Wilson to see how the parrot responded.

Theresa let out a long shriek that was so high-pitched Harriet clamped her fingers tighter over her ears.

"Whoa," Harriet said when she stopped.

"Yeah. And you knew it was coming. That sound yanked me out of a dead sleep this morning."

The door burst open to reveal Polly and a leashed Murphy with worry on both of their faces. "Is everything okay?"

"Everything is fine, Polly. Theresa was just demonstrating Wilson's latest sound effect."

"Good to know. I thought maybe one of you had gotten hurt somehow."

Wilson repeated the same shrill sound, and Murphy growled.

Polly reached for the door. "Sorry. I'm getting him out."

Harriet rocked back on her heels. "Interesting. It's not often that an animal reacts to a sound the way Murphy just did. Usually, they respond by shaking, panting, pacing, hiding, running to their owner, or even self-mutilating. But growling?"

"Self-mutilating," Theresa repeated. "Like Wilson is doing with his feathers?"

"Yes. Plucking feathers is an example of self-mutilating. In a cat, it might present as excessive licking, chewing, biting, or pulling out fur. In dogs, it could be licking or chewing excessively at a particular area." Harriet watched Wilson turn his back to them both and begin to rock. "The way it manifests can be different for each animal, but there's always a reason behind the behavior."

Theresa sucked in a breath. "Could he be trying to tell us he's sick?"

"He could be, of course. But my guess is still stress. Because of the new environment, the sounds, the plucking, and the kind of behavior he's exhibiting right now, as if he's trying to hide from us."

Theresa bent down, her forehead creased with worry. "He rocks like that in the morning now. After and sometimes even during the sounds he makes."

Harriet made a few notes on her clipboard. "What time do you tend to wake up in the morning? Generally speaking?"

"Usually, I sleep in until about ten because I'm more productive late at night. But on Sundays, I get up earlier so I can go to church."

Harriet thought a moment. "Would you be opposed to me stopping by your house at the time you plan to wake up on Sunday, so I can witness the whole range of Wilson's current behaviors? It might be helpful in figuring out what's going on and possibly forming a plan to combat it."

"You mean like make a house call?" Leaning against the edge of the exam table, Theresa tugged Wilson's cage close. "I thought house calls from doctors stopped decades ago."

When Wilson's rocking ceased, yet his back remained turned even to Theresa, Harriet made another note in the bird's file. "If Wilson were a horse or a donkey or some other big farm animal, I'd go to him. If this is what he needs for me to figure out what's going on so I can help him, then it's what I want to do. Seeing him in his environment while he goes through his abnormal behaviors might help me do exactly that."

"Are you sure?" Theresa said. "I feel like it's a lot to ask."

"You're not asking. I'm offering. What time on Sunday morning would be best for me to see what I need to see and for you to still have time to get ready and out the door for church?"

"Would eight be too early to have you come?"

Harriet noted the time and day. "Not at all."

"I don't know what to say, other than thank you. Just as you got this gorgeous farm with the house, gallery, and clinic from your grandfather, I got Wilson from mine when he was a baby." Theresa's laugh disappeared as quickly as it came. "Not exactly the same thing, obviously, but he means a lot to me. Right, Wilson?"

The bird remained silent but glanced at Theresa, his head bobbing ever so slightly.

"If I have to go back home to write for Wilson's benefit, I'll do that. The cottage I'm renting isn't in the best shape, my landlord is too lazy to fix even one or two of the dozen things wrong with the place, and dogs bark from nearby yards at all hours of the day and night. Yet despite all of that and the gloomy weather, the writing is really starting to flow."

"Maybe you should suggest my handyman to your landlord. Mike does everything I've asked of him in a quarter of the time I'd expect. He built the pen in the barn, fixed a hole in the gallery roof, and now he's working on the broken window. Unfortunately, I don't think there's a thing he can do about the weather."

Theresa managed a laugh. "I'll keep praying about that then."

"Good idea." Harriet led Theresa out to the reception area. "Sunday morning should give me a better idea of everything going on with Wilson. And I'm confident that when I have that, we'll be able to figure this out and get him back to his old self once and for all."

"Thanks, Harriet."

"My pleasure." As she watched Theresa and Wilson leave, Harriet prayed that she'd be able to solve this particular mystery soon.

CHAPTER THIRTEEN

Harriet gently stroked Murphy's snout and waited for the quiet calm that usually filled her spirit at this time of day. But it didn't come. Instead, all she felt was the same uneasiness that had been building in her heart since Polly left at the end of their workday.

"None of this is your fault, dear."

"But what if it is, Aunt Jinny?" Harriet asked. "First Nessie is taken, then someone breaks into the gallery and steals Grandad's painting of her, and then someone gets into our barn and steals one of my boarders. You can't deny that this all seems to be aimed at me."

Aunt Jinny pulled Harriet into a hearty embrace. "I know none of this makes any sense. But that doesn't make it your fault."

"When the sole link between the incidents was Nessie, I could see Polly's theory that Tarquin Summerton was involved. Especially when Cindy told us he'd already picked out a name for a dog he wants," Harriet said. "I didn't like it, and I really didn't want to consider the possibility, but I couldn't discount it entirely either."

"I can. There's no way Tarquin could ignore how special that cat is to his wife."

"And then Grandad's painting of Nessie was stolen," Harriet went on.

"Oh, Harriet, you can't actually think Tarquin had anything to do with that," Aunt Jinny protested.

"Polly certainly tried to make a case for it after our last appointment. According to the grapevine, Cindy and Tarquin want another baby but can't afford to feed another mouth right now."

Aunt Jinny stared at Harriet. "And that means Tarquin would steal his wife's beloved cat, and then a painting of it?"

Harriet shrugged. "Polly tossed it out as a possibility. But I've been doing a lot of thinking, and I don't see how he would work as a viable suspect. The second he tried to sell the painting, he'd be busted."

"Exactly."

"And now Princess has been stolen too."

"But no note this time, right?"

"Correct. No note. But now, even if there was a way in which a stolen painting could be sold without consequence, Nessie is no longer the common denominator. *I* am. Besides, the note in the gallery said, 'Now you know what it's like.' That was aimed at me."

"You can't be certain of that," Aunt Jinny said.

"Maybe I couldn't then, but now that Princess has been stolen, I most definitely can." Harriet spread her arms to include their surroundings at the clinic. "I'm the target. Someone is trying to punish me specifically. It's the only thing that connects all the dots."

"Why on earth would someone target you?"

"So far, my best guess is someone who blames me for what happened to his dog."

"You think that Renner man with the bad reviews did all this?" Aunt Jinny asked, her eyes wide.

"I can't think of anyone else."

"Have you told Van your theory?"

"No. I don't want to add unfounded allegations involving the police to Dale's list of grievances against me."

"But if he's done all these things, he has to be stopped. How do you think you'll find evidence either incriminating or exonerating him?"

"I'd like to go to his house and see if there's any sign of Nessie or Princess or Grandad's painting."

"And you're just going to show up unannounced?"

"Scout's new food arrived before closing tonight. It's the perfect excuse." The food had to be specially ordered, as the company required a prescription for it. If Dale became comfortable enough to order it himself, Harriet would happily send him the prescription, but for now she'd taken the initiative to order the food and was including complimentary treats that were safe for Scout. She planned to deliver them herself. The sooner Scout was switched to the new diet, the sooner he'd begin to feel better.

"I see. In that case, please make sure you have your phone with you and that Polly knows exactly where you are when you go there. You can't be too careful."

"Polly said the same thing before she left the clinic this evening, which is why I'm keeping Murphy inside with me tonight."

"I think that's smart," Aunt Jinny said. "Now, before I go, let me take another look at your hand."

"My hand is fine. It was a little bite, and Wilson is a healthy bird."

Aunt Jinny raised an eyebrow. "A bite is a bite, as I told you when I first got here this evening."

She let Aunt Jinny peer under the recently applied bandage. "I'll make sure to put a little of Grandad's ointment on it first thing in the morning, like you said."

"Good. But clean it carefully first. And if starts showing signs of infection, call me right away, okay?"

"Yes, Aunt Jinny." Harriet pressed a kiss to her aunt's cheek and then hurried to suppress a yawn that caught her by surprise. "Maybe I'm more tired than I realize."

"Then go get some sleep. And, again, call if you need me. For anything." Aunt Jinny headed for the clinic door. "I know you're going through a hard time right now, dear. But trust that God will make it right."

"I'm trying, Aunt Jinny."

CHAPTER FOURTEEN

It was the same thing she'd witnessed in its entirety three times already that morning.

The phone rang.

Polly greeted the caller who was due to arrive at the clinic at any moment, explained that the things happening at Cobble Hill Farm were out of Harriet's control, and then, finally, reminded the caller that they could always schedule with the clinic again if they changed their mind.

"I'm sorry, Harriet." Polly set the receiver in its cradle, defeat slumping her against the back of her desk chair. "Mrs. Smythe won't be here for her appointment this morning either."

"You and Aunt Jinny keep telling me that what happened to Princess isn't my fault, but it sure seems like you're the only two who think that way." Harriet knew she was moping, but she couldn't help it.

"We keep telling you that because it's true."

"Yet people are canceling their appointments this morning." She massaged her temples. "I'm sorry, Polly. You don't deserve my frustration. I'm just desperate for a way to fix all of this. Do we have anyone coming in today at all?"

Polly blew out a sigh. "No."

"So I could leave for a while and be fine?"

"You could," Polly said.

"Let me get Charlie and Maxwell settled, and then I'll grab Scout's new food and treats to take over to Mr. Renner. While I do that, if you can text me his address, that'll be great."

Polly stood and retrieved her raincoat from the back of her chair. "I can pull it up on my phone on the way."

"You can't come." Harriet pointed at Polly's desk. "I need you here, covering the phone."

Polly slipped her arms into her coat. "I'll forward the calls to mine."

"But what about Murphy?" Harriet smiled at the dog, who clearly knew his name, since he left off sniffing a corner of the room and bounded toward her. "Who, by the way, is ready for a walk and some playtime, aren't you, boy?"

The clinic door swished open, and Mike stepped inside. "Hello, ladies."

"Hey, Mike," Harriet and Polly said in unison.

"I finished up with the trim around the gallery window and thought I should check in and see if there's anything else I can do."

Polly pounced. "Could you hold down the fort here for a little while so Harriet and I can run an errand?"

"I'd be happy to, but I know absolutely nothing about computers."

"You don't have to. We need you to hang out with Murphy," Polly said. "Take him for a nice long walk, rub his tummy when he shows it to you—that sort of thing."

"Oh, that's easy. Consider it done."

Harriet waved Mike's answer away. "Mike, I can't ask you to do that."

"Nonsense." Mike squatted down as Murphy trotted in his direction for a sniff and a pet.

"I hired you to make things work around here," Harriet protested. "Not to walk dogs."

Mike scratched the eager Labrador beneath the chin. "You do realize Murphy isn't just *any* dog, right?"

"What do you mean?"

He paused in scratching Murphy's neck to greet Maxwell and Charlie. "I talked out several issues with him while I was building the roaming pen in the barn. He's a bona fide therapist."

"Many dogs are." Harriet chuckled. "Mike, I have to thank you for everything you've been doing around here. It seems you're always right there to help when the unthinkable happens, and I appreciate it."

Mike gave each animal one last pet and then stood. "I just wish I could've been there *before* the unthinkable happened."

"I do as well. But I'm still grateful to you, Mike."

"It's my pleasure, Doc, as is spending a little time with Murphy while the two of you do whatever it is you need to do."

Polly poked Harriet when she hesitated. "Come on, boss. Let's go put an end to this, once and for all."

"If it's him."

"Him?" Mike echoed.

"The person responsible for everything that's gone wrong around here this past week," Polly said.

"The police will find whoever that is," Mike replied.

Harriet clicked her tongue, summoning Maxwell and Charlie. "I can't sit back and wait for that. There may be nothing left of this clinic by the time that happens. It's a chance I can't afford to take."

Harriet drove the Land Rover through the narrow streets of White Church Bay. She passed Galloway's General Store, the White Hart inn and restaurant, Tales & Treasures book and toy shop, and Cliffside Chippy, the smells from the latter making her and Polly's stomachs growl in unison.

"Do you want to stop and get something to eat on the way?" Harriet asked.

Polly waved the suggestion away. "I'd prefer a spot of tea afterward. When we have something to celebrate."

"We don't know it's him, Polly."

"I think we do. He's the only one who makes sense for all of this."

"What about Tarquin?"

"He made sense until he didn't."

Harriet continued on, driving them past the Crow's Nest. "I was so lost in what happened with Princess yesterday morning that I never thought to ask how the rest of your darts game went. Did you and Mike end up winning?"

"We did," Polly said.

"I imagine the fact that it was *you* made the loss even worse for Mr. Renner."

"I can't say one way or the other. He was already in a surly mood from all the empathy you were getting after that evening's newscast."

"I'm sorry for that, Polly. But congratulations on your win. Well done."

"It would have been more satisfying if we'd had a worthy opponent," Polly replied. "Theo nearly hit the waitress in the shoulder with a dart at one point during our game."

Harriet slowed to let a pedestrian cross. "Yikes."

"Fortunately, the waitress dodged, and he missed." Polly pointed at a man hurrying down the street as the temporary pause in the day's drizzle came to an end. "Speaking of Theo, that's him."

The drizzle quickly gave way to an all-out downpour, sending people running for cars, open shops, or whatever shelter they could find. Polly's fellow darts player quickened his pace.

"Let's offer him a ride," Harriet said, slowing even more.

"All right." Polly rolled down her window and called to him.

The man swiped at his face with the sleeve of his jacket and peered toward them, his expression changing from recognition to irritation as his gaze moved from Polly to Harriet.

"Would you like a ride to your car?" Polly asked.

Theo stepped closer. "I don't have a car. I'm walking."

"Then we could drop you off wherever you're going."

He squinted against yet another uptick in rain. "Why would you do that?"

"Um, because it's raining?" Polly replied. "And because my friend is nice."

The man glared up at the sky then said, "I'm out on Rocky Shore Drive."

"That's right around the corner from where we're going," Polly told Harriet.

"Perfect." She would have taken him there even if it had been on the opposite side of town. "Get in, Theo."

He climbed into the back, shaking his hair free of rain as he did.

Polly twisted in her seat. "I'm Polly Thatcher, in case you don't remember."

"I remember. You're the one I let beat me at darts the other night."

Harriet grinned. "And I'm Harriet Bailey."

"I know who you are."

Thrown by the man's clipped response, Harriet tossed a pointed look at Polly before glancing at Theo in the rearview mirror, her mind racing to place him. "Have we met before?"

He stared out the window. "No. But like I said, I know who you are."

Polly shifted into place in her own seat and motioned for Harriet to continue driving. "He was at the Crow's Nest when Candace Moore's report on the gallery break-in aired."

A snort came from the back seat.

"And he was Dale Renner's partner that night, remember?" Polly addressed Theo again. "For what it's worth, his dog has a major food sensitivity, and ignoring it could be dangerous for Scout's health. Doctor Bailey would never make up a diagnosis to trick people into giving her more money."

Harriet glanced into the rearview mirror again but saw no response to Polly's words. "Let it go, Polly," she whispered. "It doesn't matter."

"It does if it's going to make people judge you unfairly, especially when you're going out of your way to be kind to them." Polly straightened in her seat. "See that, Harriet? Another one of Nessie's signs is on that tree."

Sure enough, midway up a gray willow tree, a rain-soaked flyer showcased the familiar feline above the words HAVE YOU SEEN ME?

"Grandad would be so upset if he were here," Harriet said. "He may have been the one to rescue her all those years ago, but I think their journey together ended up rescuing him in return."

"No, Felix Burton rescued Nessie," Theo said sharply.

"Felix Burton *spotted* Nessie," Harriet corrected gently. "My grandfather rescued her."

"Semantics, wouldn't you say? Seeing as how the second couldn't have happened without the first."

"Of course." She pinned Polly with a questioning eye as she continued to direct her response at the man in the back seat. "Did you know Felix Burton?"

"I knew of him."

"Theo and Max were talking to Doug and Candace the other night at the Crow's Nest," Polly said. "Clearly, Candace has done some digging and shared what she found with the two people she could tell would lap it up."

Harriet shot her friend a warning glance.

"Since I think it's important for a person to be informed, I'm going to do some informing, Theo," Polly said, her voice void of its usual warmth. "Are you ready?"

"I can hardly wait," Theo said with a sneer.

Polly spun around in her seat. "What's your problem, Theo?"

"Based on what I saw on the news the other night, *I'm* not the one with the problem."

"Apparently you are," Polly argued. "You were surrounded by dozens of people who spoke well of Harriet the other night. Yet you chose to decide that the one naysayer in the entire place was the one to believe. Why? So you can have someone to play a game with? I feel sorry for you."

"I don't need your pity."

"You have it anyway. We've reached your road. Which house?"

He pointed. "That one."

Harriet pulled to a stop in front of the old gray cottage he indicated. Before she could think of anything else to say, he was gone, dodging raindrops en route to his front door. When he reached it, he glared at them for a moment and then disappeared inside.

"What on earth was that?" Harriet demanded.

"A sterling example of someone who needs a crash course in picking friends. And he 'let' us win? Seriously? I can't wait to tell Mike that when we get back to the clinic."

"I was talking about you too, Polly," Harriet said. "You were goading him. I doubt you won him over to my side that way."

"I don't care. I'm not going to let misinformation keep spreading about you. He needed to know the truth."

"We should also give grace. After all, isn't Theo new to White Church Bay?" Harriet asked.

"I heard him tell Dale he moved here last month." Polly scowled at her. "Are you asking because of the Felix stuff? I told you Dale was talking to Candace and Doug that night. I assumed he was unloading on her about Scout, but if Candace is as sharp as I think she is, she's talking to everyone in this town she can. Which means she's heard rumors about Felix and the part he played in Nessie's story, and she wanted to see if Dale could add any more fuel to that flame. Theo probably heard about Felix from her."

Harriet pressed her lips together then said, "Aunt Jinny said Grandad was good about giving Felix props for being the one who first spotted Nessie in those rocks. And that it was the media who always cut him from the story."

"That doesn't surprise me, but some people like to believe the uglier version of things, even if it's not true. Dale's house is right up there, the first house on the right."

"Got it."

"And not to tempt fate, but I think the rain has stopped," Polly added.

"Perfect timing." Harriet slowed in front of a mailbox bearing the name D. RENNER and turned in to the small, narrow driveway. She cut the engine behind a parked sedan and stared up at the house. "On one hand, it would be good if everything that's happened is because of him. Because then we'd know, and it would stop, and everything could be fixed."

"And on the other hand?" Polly prompted.

"On the other hand, I don't want it to be him at all. I want him to be able to deal with Scout's diagnosis in a healthy way." She rested her head against the back of her seat. "I could even help him with it."

Polly reached down between her feet and lifted the bag of special food onto her lap. "There's only one way to find out which it will be, especially since you don't want to involve the police unnecessarily."

"And I still don't want to."

"So, are you ready?"

With a haste that belied the dread she felt, Harriet scooped up the bag of treats, made her way around the front of the Land Rover, and met Polly on the walkway. When they reached the door, Polly knocked then pointed to a window. "There's a light on in there. Probably means he's home."

"Between that and the car we parked behind, I think that's a safe guess. Whether he opens the door to us, though, isn't."

The sound of a small engine reached them from behind the house. Polly trotted along the side and peered around the corner. "Oh, I see him. He's in the back garden with some sort of electric hedge trimmer. My mum would lecture him on trimming wet plants."

Harriet followed Polly. "If that's where he is, that's where we'll go."

Polly tapped her ear. "I hear dogs."

"Yes, but the sound is coming from way over there." Harriet gestured toward the yards beyond Dale's.

He caught sight of them and killed the trimmer's engine with an angry jab at a button. "What are you doing here?" he growled.

"We've brought some things to help Scout transition to his new diet."

A series of rapid, muffled barks from somewhere in the distance drowned out her last few words.

She willed herself to step closer. "I know this is hard. And I'm so very, very sorry about this whole situation." She took a deep breath. "But you have to know you can still give Scout a good life. It'll be more expensive than you expected, and you'll have to be careful about what he eats, but he can be healthy and happy for a long time. I promise."

Dale's frown deepened. "That's easy for you to say. You don't have to refigure your finances to come up with a way to afford all this. You probably have all the money in the world, but you still want mine, huh? Do you get a cut from the dog food manufacturer when you diagnose an animal with this 'allergy' and tell people they have to pay for this specialized diet?"

Polly bristled. "Dr. Bailey did not make any of this up, Mr. Renner. You can see that for yourself if you'd read the report. It shows what Scout's sample reacted to and even explains how to read the result."

Dale set the electric trimmer down at his feet, pulled off his gloves, and locked eyes with Harriet. "He was a perfect dog when I brought him in to that clinic on that compound of yours. I wanted you to help him because he was sick, and instead you want to drain my savings. And I'm supposed to believe he has some deficiency I've never heard of after owning dogs my entire life?"

"I completely understand why you're upset," Harriet said. "This is sad and stressful all around. If it helps, I've been looking into programs that can provide discounts and financial aid for situations like this, and I'm happy to—"

"Spare me your charity," Dale said through gritted teeth.

She laid a calming hand on Polly's arm before her friend could give the sharp retort she clearly meant to. "If you'd like, Mr. Renner, I can ask that the report be forwarded to a vet of your choosing. That would enable you to discuss the results with an independent third party."

"Scout will still be sick, won't he?" Dale snapped.

"Yes," Polly said. "But then you'll see that Dr. Bailey isn't to blame and she isn't lying to you. She's not at fault for this."

Harriet shifted the bag of treats in her arms. "And neither are you, Mr. Renner."

His anger faltered against a flash of pain. "I always share a bit of my dinner with him. Meat pies, roast chicken, all of it. He loves it. Whenever I cook, he sprawls in the doorway and watches me. I call him my little sous-chef. And now I can't bond with him that way anymore."

"That's not true, actually," Harriet said. "It's merely a matter of switching what you share with him. Don't give him meat or anything that's touched meat, but you can still share dog-safe fruits and vegetables with him. Lots of dogs love those things. You could also try giving him natural peanut butter. There are still plenty of ways for you to bond with and spoil him, I promise. We'll just need to be a little more creative."

Dale raised an eyebrow at her. "We?"

Harriet nodded. "I'm not going to leave you to deal with this alone. This is a massive shift in Scout's life, and in yours. I'm here for whatever you need to make it happen in the way that makes you most comfortable."

Dale took the food from Polly, swallowing hard. "This is a huge thing. I've been feeling overwhelmed by it all, and I don't think I've dealt with it as well as I could have." He raised his head. "Thank you. I'm sorry I've been so rotten to you."

"I understand," Harriet assured him.

Dale studied the bag of dog food. "Okay, do I need to do a gradual transition with this, like I would if I were switching Scout to a normal dog food?"

"That's usually the case," Harriet said, impressed. Dale was an attentive pet owner, and she appreciated that. "However, since his old food is what's causing the problem, I would prefer if you did the switch all at once. He should feel better sooner that way."

Dale nodded and accepted the treats from her. "I'll go do that right now."

"If you need anything, please call me. Day or night. I'm here to listen and give any guidance I can. You don't have to face this by yourself."

He gave her a small smile. "Thanks, Doc."

As she and Polly made their way back to the Land Rover, Harriet found herself hoping that if Dale Renner could call her by her grandfather's nickname, perhaps more clients would come to trust her that much as well.

CHAPTER FIFTEEN

Y ou didn't ask him about Nessie, or Princess, or Doc Bailey's painting," Polly blurted the second they were inside the Land Rover.

Harriet carefully backed out of the driveway onto the road.
"You're right, I didn't."

"But that's why we were there, isn't it?" Polly asked. "To see if
our sole suspect is actually the culprit?"

"We were there to take him Scout's new food."

"Okay, but I don't understand why we left without getting any
answers," Polly protested.

"Because after that conversation, I believe that if he's behind
everything that's happened, he's going to do the right thing."

Polly crossed her arms in front of her seat belt. "And why do you
think that?"

"He heard me there at the end. I saw it in his eyes. I'd like to give
him a little time to make things right if he's responsible for what's
happened."

"If he has Nessie and Princess, whose owners are beside themselves missing their pets, you want to give him *time*?"

"A man who loves his dog the way Dale Renner loves Scout
doesn't have it in him to harm any animal. I'm certain of that. I'm
also certain that if he is the person who took them, they—and

Grandad's painting—will reappear. He'll understand that he's hurting people who love their pets the way he loves his, and he'll realize he doesn't want to be that person."

"And if they do reappear, you're simply going to let it go?" Polly asked.

"That's not my call with the missing pets. But maybe I could ask the police to go easy on him about the painting if he returns it. I can't control whether they press criminal charges, but I won't be pressing any."

Harriet glanced at the dashboard clock. "Do you think we could check in on Cindy Summerton before we get back to the clinic?"

"Definitely," Polly replied. "My phone hasn't rung at all since we left."

Harriet took a deep breath and released it. "Do you think Mike will mind if we take a little more time?"

"I doubt it, but I'll text him to be sure if that'll make you feel better. Mike's a good bloke, Harriet. He likes to help."

"I know," Harriet said. "But I'd still like to ask, to be considerate."

"And to check in on Murphy?" Polly asked with a knowing smile.

Harriet opened her mouth to protest but gave up and said instead, "It's almost scary how well you know me, Polly."

Drawing in a deep, steadying breath, Harriet knocked on the Summertons' door.

"What an idyllic little play area."

Harriet followed Polly's gaze to the far side of the front porch and took in the barely knee-high slide and the soft landing pad at its base. "It is," she agreed. Not that she was surprised that Cindy would make sure her child had a wonderful life after how well she'd cared for Nessie for the past six years.

She knocked again, a bit louder.

Polly rested her hands on her hips. "I don't know how they make doors in the States, but around here, you can knock harder than that, boss."

Harriet chuckled. "Emerson could be napping. Or maybe they're out. I didn't see a car in the driveway."

Polly indicated a window. "There's a telly on in there. I can see it flickering through the curtain."

Harriet knocked again.

Moments later, she heard footsteps on the other side of the door.

"Dr. Bailey!" Cindy exclaimed as she opened the door. "Has Nessie been found? Is—is she okay?"

Harriet held up her hands. "No, Cindy, I'm sorry. I don't have any news on Nessie. I just wanted to check on you."

"I thought maybe you'd gotten a call because of her chip." Pressing her hand to her chest, Cindy slumped. "Every time the phone rings, I think it's someone calling to tell me they've spotted her. Every time someone comes to the door, I think they're going to have Nessie in their arms. But the longer this goes on, the more I'm starting to wonder if I should brace myself for the very real possibility that I'll never see her again."

"Mama!"

Cindy glanced over her shoulder then waved Harriet and Polly inside. "Please. Come in. Make yourself comfortable while I fetch Emerson."

"We don't want to intrude," Harriet protested. "We just wanted to see how you're doing."

"You're not intruding at all. I've been afraid to leave the house when Tarquin is at work lest I miss news about Nessie or she manages to find her way home." Cindy stepped back to allow them in and then closed the door behind them. "You can wait in here while I tend to Emerson. It won't take me more than a few minutes."

"Of course. Take your time," Polly assured her.

Cindy disappeared down a narrow hallway toward the rear of the young family's modest home. A quiet click in the distance was followed, seconds later, by Cindy's voice, crisp and clear. "Did you have a good rest, Emerson?"

"It sounds like she's still here in the room," Polly whispered.

Harriet pointed to a small white box on the mantel. "It's the baby monitor."

Polly hopped up and plucked a few stuffed animals off the top of the couch.

"What are you doing?" Harriet asked.

"These need to be sorted." Polly carried them to a nearby toy chest and lined them up, by size, across its lid. When she was done, she gathered up a few more toys from the hearth and sorted them by color in front of the stuffed animals.

"You really can't help yourself, can you?" Harriet teased.

Polly continued around the room, organizing discarded toys as she went. "I don't know what you're talking about."

"Yes you do."

Polly set the last toy in place, surveyed the room, and then claimed a spot on the couch. "I don't sit still well. Especially when I see a way I can help."

Harriet's laugh mingled with a sweet, high-pitched one from Emerson through the monitor.

"Do you want that one day?" Polly asked, tilting her head toward the device.

"A baby?" At Polly's nod, Harriet coughed to clear her throat of a sudden tightness. "I did. And then my ex-fiancé broke off our engagement and I came here. I've been too busy building a new life to think about it much."

"His loss is our gain."

"Not that you're biased or anything," Harriet said, studying the series of framed photographs lined up across the mantel. Pictures of Emerson, of Cindy and Tarquin on their wedding day, and one of Cindy holding Nessie.

"I remember that moment like it was yesterday."

Harriet spun to face Cindy. "Was this the day Grandad gave her to you?"

"It was." Cindy bounced Emerson on her hip. "I don't remember who took that picture. I was so focused on the feel of Nessie in my arms and the overwhelming relief that I was no longer alone. That someone would be happy to see me when I walked in the door, like Mum had always been."

The photo bore out her words. Love was so evident on Cindy's face as she smiled down at the kitten in her arms. But Harriet found herself drinking in the sight of her grandfather, watching it all from the background of the photo. She would always miss him.

"I know your grandfather loved Nessie. I can't imagine how hard it must have been for him to hand her over to me all those years ago. But that's the kind of person Doc Bailey was—always doing for others."

Harriet blinked back tears at Cindy's description. "He was the best," she managed to say past the lump in her throat. "I loved every moment I got to spend with him when I was growing up. The visits, the phone calls, the letters, everything. And I know from what he told me that he wanted Nessie to make her home with you."

"I loved Nessie," Cindy said, her voice breaking. "No, I *love* Nessie. Because I'm not giving up on her."

"Ness," Emerson cooed.

"Yes, sweetheart," Cindy said, laying her cheek against her son's head and closing her eyes. "I know you miss Nessie too."

Harriet studied the photo once more. Cindy's obvious joy. Young Nessie's curiosity and trust. The quiet kindness on her grandfather's face as he soaked in the moment.

"Cindy?" Harriet asked. "Can I see where Nessie was taken from last Friday?"

"Of course. This way." Cindy led the way to the patio door and peeked outside. "When the sun is shining, the garden is a wonderful place to be. But even now, after a rain, it's still lovely."

She opened the door and stepped out onto a narrow walkway. Harriet followed, but Polly stayed inside, likely not wanting to risk the rain returning without warning and soaking her. Various shrubs and plants grew all around, their leaves dappled with raindrops. Up ahead, beneath a small wooden archway, sat a bistro table with two chairs. On the ground beside it was a food dish. Empty.

"I haven't sat at that table since that day," Cindy said. "I just can't. This was our favorite spot—mine for reading and having a cup of tea during Emerson's nap, and Nessie's for exploring and enjoying the occasional ray of sunshine."

"You were out here together that day?" Harriet asked.

Cindy bit her lip. "There was always a bit of time after Emerson woke from his nap when Nessie would be out here by herself. I called it her 'alone time.' She needed it after I had Emerson."

"A lot of people don't realize that adding a small human to a family means an adjustment period for the pets who already live there."

"Nessie had some jealousy after Emerson was born," Cindy said. "She didn't mind Tarquin becoming part of the mix, probably because he came with a lap big enough for her. But when Emerson came along, she had to share my time, my affection, and my lap— something I began to realize was a problem. She'd gone from being the center of my world to being almost a living prop overnight. She wasn't aggressive toward the baby or anything like that, but I could tell she was depressed about it."

"That can be tough," Harriet agreed, having seen such situations before.

"So I made naptime Nessie time, where I reminded her that she was still important to me. Then, when Emerson was up from his nap, I would leave her out here by herself for thirty or forty minutes so she got a longer break from him. Babies can be a little more handsy than she's used to. She was as attached to me as I was to her, so I never worried about her being out here alone." Cindy blinked hard. "Until a week ago, that is."

"You came up with a good solution that helped everyone. It's not your fault someone took advantage of it." Harriet pointed to the back gate. "May I poke around?"

"Of course."

Harriet followed the narrow, winding walkway to its end at a shoulder-high gate. "I'm guessing the police think whoever took her let himself in this way?"

Cindy switched Emerson to her other hip. "They do."

Harriet peered across the top of the gate at the yards on either side. "And I'm guessing none of your neighbors reported seeing anyone unusual lurking around your gate that day?"

"They didn't."

"Do you know them well?" Harriet asked.

"By face, mostly. I take Emerson for walks in his pram sometimes." Cindy kissed Emerson's temple. "But not this week, right, my love? This week we've not gone anywhere with the pram. I just can't make myself leave. The few times I have—when Tarquin has been home—it's to drive around, hoping I'll catch a glimpse of her wherever she's being held."

The patio door opened, and Polly stepped out, an odd expression on her face. "Harriet?"

"Oh, Polly!" Cindy hurried to meet her. "I forgot you were inside. I'm so sorry."

"No, no, it's okay." Polly's gaze traveled to Harriet's even though her words were directed at Cindy. "I think you missed a call from your husband just now."

"Thanks for letting me know. I'll call him back in a bit."

"Harriet," Polly said, a hint of urgency in her voice. "We need to head out."

"Did someone call? Is there an emergency?"

"I'll explain as we go." Polly jerked her head toward the door. "Time has gotten away from us, it seems."

Polly's gaze remained fixed on Harriet's as they followed Cindy and Emerson into the house. Harriet couldn't begin to guess what her friend was trying to tell her.

A jolt of fear rocketed through her body so strongly that she had to steady herself against the wall before continuing her trek down the hall to the front door. More than anything, she wanted to shake Polly, to ask her what was wrong, to hear that Murphy was okay, that Mike was okay, that nothing else had gone horribly wrong. But she had to wait.

She liked Cindy, but it was torture to stand by through the goodbyes to learn what Polly wanted to tell her.

The moment they climbed into the Land Rover, Harriet turned on her. "So what is it? Why did we have to leave all of a sudden?"

"It's Doc Bailey's painting." Polly cast a glance at Cindy's closed front door. "The swiped one."

"Did Van call? Did the police find it?"

"No. I heard Tarquin's voice and thought I'd been caught. So I just ran out. I'm sorry. I should have held my nerve."

"Caught doing what? And what does Tarquin's voice have to do with Grandad's painting?" Harriet demanded.

Again, Polly took in the Summertons' home. "I was going to join you in the back garden, but I stopped for a moment to check a text message from Van. And then I was walking past Emerson's nursery and I saw that Cindy had left the wipes container open on the changing table. I didn't want them to dry out, so I stepped in to shut it. But when I pushed the door open enough to walk inside, it bumped into something. I peeked around it to see if I'd hurt anything and that was when I heard Tarquin's voice."

"I didn't realize he was home," Harriet said.

"He wasn't, but I thought he had come in the front door and would think I was snooping." Polly drummed her fingers against her thigh. "So I ducked into the hallway and hurried to the back door. By the time I realized I had heard his voice on the answering machine and that he wasn't actually there, I was too spooked to return to the nursery and see for sure if I was right."

"About what?" Harriet asked.

"If I did actually see the painting of Nessie behind the nursery door."

Harriet gaped at her friend. "What?"

Polly held up her hands. "I don't know for certain. It was behind the door with a blanket covering it. But it was the right size. And what little of it I could see—well, the frame matched."

"That's a very serious accusation, Polly," Harriet said.

"I know, but I think I should text Van and tell him what I saw. What if it's a lead? I don't want to miss a chance to get that painting back."

"You don't know it was Grandad's painting for certain," Harriet pointed out.

"I don't. But it might be."

"We can't have the police descending on Cindy's house because you *might* have seen it," Harriet protested. "Not when she has a little one in the house. It'd be too frightening for him. And she's going through enough right now."

Polly tapped her phone's screen. "That doesn't give them the right to keep a stolen painting."

"If it is Grandad's painting, why would they take it? And how?"

Polly set her phone on her lap. "The *how* for them would be the same how for anyone. They, probably Tarquin, would have broken into the gallery either late Tuesday night or very early Wednesday morning and swiped it. Or maybe they even did it together."

Harriet played out Polly's words in her thoughts, her mind's eye trying to place Tarquin and Cindy in a scene where a chair was used to break a window that one, or both of them, subsequently crawled through empty-handed and back out afterward with a framed painting. Then again, Polly had a point. Someone had done exactly what she was trying to imagine—and done it successfully.

"And as for the *why,* maybe Tarquin took the painting to give to Cindy as a way to alleviate his guilt for having taken Nessie," Polly said. "And maybe, when he realized the painting increased in value because of it, he thought he could make money from it—money that might make it easier for them to have another baby."

"A baby he'd never see because he'd be in jail."

"Then maybe the motive is wrong," Polly argued. "But if what I saw is Nessie's painting, then Tarquin must have had some reason to take it."

Harriet started to argue again but stopped. Polly was as familiar with the painting as Harriet was. If she thought she'd seen it, Harriet had no reason to doubt her. And if Polly was right about the painting, it must have come into the Summertons' house somehow. Polly's theory about it was as good as any about why the cat and the artwork had both disappeared within days of each other.

"But then how does Princess figure into this?" Harriet asked. "She has no connection to Nessie."

Polly shrugged. "There wasn't a note left with Princess either, like there was with Nessie and the painting. Which might mean Princess's disappearance is unrelated."

"But she was taken from the barn on my property," Harriet reminded her. "Twenty-four hours after the gallery was broken into. I don't think that timing could be coincidental."

"I understand that, but can we consider the possibility that the two Nessie-related crimes are unrelated to Princess? Because your grandfather's painting might be behind Emerson's door right now."

"But don't you think that if it was, Cindy would know? That she'd call the police or reach out to me the second she saw it?"

"Cindy has had a lot of loss in her life. Her father. Her mother. Now Nessie. Maybe she can't handle the thought of losing Tarquin to jail."

Harriet's stomach began to churn. "Oh, Polly, I don't want to think this could be true. I really don't."

"I know. And maybe it's not. But maybe Van could get a search warrant and find out for sure," Polly said.

"He can't search without probable cause. And I'm pretty sure us telling him that there's something about the same size with maybe the same frame as Grandad's painting behind Emerson's bedroom door wouldn't qualify."

"Then what do we do?"

"I guess I'll have to go back in and see for myself whether it's truly Grandad's painting."

"How? Are you going to ring the bell and tell her you want to check behind Emerson's door?" Polly asked. "Because I think that might raise some questions."

Harriet pushed open her door and slid out from behind the steering wheel. "Honestly? I should've used the restroom when I was inside."

Polly reached for her own door handle. "Then I should come too."

"That will seem more suspicious."

At Polly's nod, Harriet pushed the door closed and hurried to the front door, where she knocked again.

The door swung open, and Cindy peered out. "Dr. Bailey, you're back. Is everything okay?"

"Everything is fine. Polly and I had to go over a few things before we pulled away, and then—well, I wanted to see if I could use your loo before we head out?"

"The loo?" After a moment of hesitation that Harriet didn't think she imagined, Cindy opened the door the rest of the way. "Um…sure. It's down the hall, second door on the left."

"Got it. Thank you."

She started down the hall with Cindy on her heels. At the entrance to the living room, when Cindy veered off to be with Emerson, Harriet continued, the feel of Cindy's eyes on her back every bit as tangible as the rapid beating of her own heart.

When she reached the correct door, she glanced over her shoulder, saw Cindy watching her, and ducked inside the bathroom. She pulled out her phone and texted Polly.

I'M NOT SURE HOW TO GET TO EMERSON'S DOOR WITHOUT BEING QUESTIONED.

Polly's reply appeared after a few seconds. ALL THE SUSPENSE HAS MADE MY THROAT DRY. I'LL COME ASK FOR A GLASS OF WATER.

Before Harriet could ask what she meant, the doorbell chimed. Harriet pressed her ear to the bathroom door and listened. Sure enough, she heard Polly asking for a glass of water, followed by the sound of a cabinet opening in the kitchen.

As quickly and quietly as possible, Harriet stepped into the hallway, made sure no one could see her, then continued to the nursery door. She pushed it open and saw a crib, a changing table, and a rocking chair. She heard a faucet being turned on at the front of the house, letting her know her time was limited.

She took a step into the nursery, poked her head around the door, and caught her breath at the sight of the blanket-covered object on the other side. She froze, her mind spinning with what-ifs.

What if it was Grandad's painting?

What if it wasn't?

Polly's loud voice reached her. "Oh, thank you for the water, Cindy. I can't believe how parched I was."

Before she lost her nerve, Harriet reached around the door, grabbed the blanket, and gave a good yank.

CHAPTER SIXTEEN

Maybe it was the cold, damp air she'd run through on the way in and out of Cindy Summerton's house—twice. Maybe it was the cancellation of the clinic's last two scheduled appointments for the day. Or maybe it was a mixture of both, with the added toppings of worry, fear, and uncertainty. But whatever the reason, Harriet simply couldn't shake the chill she felt down to her toes, despite the hot tea Polly had insisted they get at the Happy Cup Tearoom & Bakery.

"You look positively gutted."

Harriet set her teacup back on its saucer and tried to make her answering smile as genuine as possible. "I'm not upset, Polly. Not about the painting behind Emerson's door anyway. Truthfully, I'm glad it wasn't Grandad's, because that would have brought with it a whole different set of problems and worries."

"I suppose." Polly took a sip of tea and grinned. "My thirst worked well to buy you time to check, didn't it?"

"It did indeed."

"I'm glad. I drank as slowly as I could."

"Well, if the clinic ends up closing, maybe Van could get you on with the police department," Harriet said glumly.

Polly rolled her eyes. "The clinic is not going to close, Harriet."

"Every single appointment we had today canceled." Harriet wrapped her cold fingers around the steaming cup. "I can't stay open if that continues."

Polly pushed a plate of banoffee pie toward Harriet. "I think you need to eat some of that. Things will look better once you do."

Harriet took a bite of the pie and hummed. "You're right. This is amazing." She'd had the tearoom's banoffee pie before, but somehow it tasted better today. Perhaps it was that the warm flavors of toffee and banana and the soft whipped cream contrasted so sharply with the rotten weather outside and the despair in her own heart. Perhaps the pastry chef had done something new. Either way, the pie was a balm to her soul.

"Eventually, you'll learn that I'm usually right," Polly teased with a wink. "And maybe you'll take my advice more often."

"If your advice is about desserts, I'll take it." Harriet savored another bite. "I wonder how someone came up with this pie."

"Two mates invented it more than fifty years ago in a restaurant in East Sussex. They called it banoffee pie in honor of its two main flavors."

"Banoffee pie," Harriet repeated, setting her fork on the empty plate. "Very clever and so delicious."

Polly stacked Harriet's plate with her own and set the stack to one side. "Feeling better now?"

"A bit, yeah. I'm sorry for being such a downer, Polly."

"You can be down. You've earned that right with everything that's been going on. But you can't let it defeat you. That's not your way, and it won't solve anything. A spoonful of sugar always helps."

Harriet poured herself a fresh cup of tea from the floral pot on the table then stirred in a sugar cube and a splash of cream. "I felt like we were finally gaining traction with the clinic. Word was getting out that I actually know what I'm doing. That Grandad had faith in me and my ability as a veterinarian for good reason."

"All of that is still true."

"But then along comes Dale's reviews claiming I'm a charlatan and this new wave of anonymous one-star reviews that say nothing but are tanking my overall rating. My boarder is stolen." Harriet took a sip of tea, trying in vain to calm herself. "And now everyone is canceling their appointments."

"It's one Friday, Harriet."

"And one Saturday too, based on the messages you just checked, remember?"

"Saturday is always a short day."

"What difference does that make?" Harriet countered. "Both of our appointments still canceled."

Polly glanced at her watch. "Our Saturday doesn't start for another eighteen hours. And if you're right about Dale, then Nessie and Princess will be back."

"I hope I'm right."

"If you're not, Van will get involved," Polly replied. "Either way, I think you need another piece of pie."

Harriet forced a laugh. "Although a part of me wants to say yes, I'll decline. But thank you. I clearly needed this far more than I realized."

"The two of you look to be deep in conversation."

Startled, Harriet snapped her head up, and her stomach dropped at the sight of a familiar blond reporter and a scruffy cameraman standing a few feet behind. "Oh, Candace, Doug. I didn't see you come in."

"We've been here a while, planning our next steps and our next stops." Candace indicated their drinks and their empty plates. "But if I'd known you were here, I'd have sprung for your tab."

"We may not be on the telly, but we can afford pie and a cuppa," Polly said, straightening with indignation.

"I didn't mean it that way. It's just—oh! I'm sorry." Candace pulled a ringing phone from her pocket, stared at the name on the screen, and then lifted wide eyes to Doug. "It's Dave Holden!"

Doug handed her a set of keys. "Take the call in the van, where it's quiet. I'll wait here until you text me to come out."

"I will." Candace made a beeline for the front door. "Wish me luck!" she called over her shoulder before she raced outside.

"She seemed chuffed," Polly observed.

"I would be too, if I were her. If that call goes as well as she hopes, she'll be wanting to buy you more than a piece of pie and a cuppa, Dr. Bailey."

"Me?" Harriet asked. "I don't understand. Who is Dave Holden?"

"One of the major execs at the station. Your stories are getting Candace a lot of attention. And she deserves it. She's been doing great work, covering everything that's been going on around here. Viewers are sticking with the program all the way to the end to hear her report, and the station's inbox is flooded with emails asking about Nessie, the painting, and now the other animal too."

"Princess," Harriet supplied.

Doug's brow furrowed. "What?"

"The other missing animal's name is Princess."

"Right." The cameraman slid his hands into the front pockets of his jeans and rocked back on his worn work boots. "Our viewership has increased every day this week. Because of Candace's coverage of you."

Polly nodded. "That makes sense. She did a report featuring Nessie on Sunday night. On Tuesday she did one about the uptick in gallery visitors that resulted from Nessie's abduction. Then the report she did on the break-in at the gallery on Wednesday had everyone in the Crow's Nest talking about Harriet's grandfather and Nessie. She's been keeping the story in the public eye from multiple angles, which is really smart."

"Do you know if Candace came across the name Felix Burton in her research this week?" Harriet asked Doug.

"She did."

"And?"

"She didn't think it was a road worth going down. It wasn't six years ago, and it isn't now." He shrugged. "And clearly, she made the right call. What's happening now is about Nessie, the poly-whatever, her—"

"Polydactyl," Harriet corrected.

Doug brushed the word away. "It's about Nessie, her painting, you and your grandfather, Princess, and people's reactions to all those things. And assuming nothing else comes up between now and broadcast time tonight, it'll be the impact of Princess's dog-napping on a business that was left to you by the late Harold Bailey. The man who found and rescued Nessie as a kitten, who painted the picture of her that's now missing, and who started and successfully ran—for decades—the practice you now call your own and seem to have managed to allow to fall apart in a matter of months. We've driven by your clinic a few times today and noticed the car park is totally empty. It's not hard to guess why."

Harriet closed her eyes, suddenly wishing she could disappear.

"If it wasn't for all this, Candace would still be just another field reporter assigned to a handful of little towns where nothing news-worthy ever happens," Doug continued. "Cats go missing everywhere, all the time. That isn't news. But a kidnapped cat and a ransom note? Her instincts told her she had something when she read it in the police blotter. It helps that it was a slow day, even for local news, when she asked to run with it. But that doesn't matter now."

Harriet clenched her jaw then took a deep breath and said, "The gallery break-in would've been newsworthy by itself. And Princess being stolen from the barn. So she would have been out here eventu-ally anyway."

"Most likely," Doug agreed. "But would those things have even happened if she hadn't gotten involved and drawn attention to White Church Bay? I'm not so sure." He pulled out his phone, read the screen, and then hooked his thumb toward the front door. "That's my cue. Enjoy the rest of your day, ladies."

And then he was gone, his stocky frame vanishing through the bakery's front door and into the gloom beyond.

"So, to paraphrase, Candace wanted to buy us pie and cuppas to thank us for all the awful things that have been going on because apparently they're making her career?" Polly stood and gathered the plates. "What a mess. Are you done with your tea?"

Harriet shook her head.

Polly carried the dishes they were finished with to the bin at the counter then returned.

"If we're wrong about Dale Renner, then who do we have?" Harriet asked her.

"No one. Unless you have a new thought?"

"It's a strange one, but maybe."

Polly leaned back in her chair. "I'm listening."

"What if everything that's happened isn't about targeting me? What if it was done for someone's gain?"

"What is there to gain from stealing a cat, a painting that everyone in the entire YTV viewing area knows was stolen, and a rather temperamental poodle?" Polly asked. "Who could possibly gain from that?"

"Hmm... I have an idea about that. Let's get back to the clinic and do something productive to give our brains a break from this. Like clean the exam rooms."

"They're clean."

"Fine. Then we can organize the files or something."

Polly raised an eyebrow at her. "They're organized."

"I forgot who I was talking to," Harriet said with a chuckle. "Then maybe we can check the living room again for the missing painting offers? If we find them, Van can check in with the people who made them."

"Sure, when we get back. But I want to hear what you're thinking."

Harriet hesitated and then perched on the edge of her seat, propping her elbows on the table's edge. "It's what Doug said about Candace."

"Which part?"

"She's getting attention from these stories," Harriet said. "Career-changing attention."

Polly pitched forward against her side of the table. "Wait. You think *she's* behind everything?"

"Maybe not everything, but some of it, to keep the story going."

"Do you really think she'd destroy your reputation to boost her own career?"

Harriet rested her head in her hands. "Hearing it said out loud is making me feel a little ridiculous."

"No, let's play this out."

"Seriously?"

"Definitely. Does it make sense that a news reporter would suddenly pick Nessie, of all animals, to catnap just to further her career? It is really out there. I mean, how would she even know the story would take off?"

"Yet my brain is going there." A few months ago, she'd suspected a different reporter of having selfish motives, though she'd been wrong.

"Next was the painting," Polly went on, as if Harriet hadn't spoken. "I suppose Candace could have had something to do with that. But you said the note that was left in the gallery was clearly from the same person who wrote the first one, right?"

"Yes."

"Yet when Princess was taken, there was no note. That still makes me think someone else was behind that." Polly sat back, frowning. "Much as I hate the idea of multiple perpetrators."

"Right. But my gut says that Nessie and Nessie's painting were taken by the same person, possibly as a way to hurt me."

"With Dale Renner being the most likely culprit," Polly said.

"I'm on the fence about that. He apologized to me and didn't act guilty of anything. And when you add in the fact there was no note when Princess was taken, the possibility that a second person is involved—a person with a very different motive—suddenly seems more likely."

"And perhaps the second person's motive was to be able to report the next big story," Polly mused. "You might have something here."

"I think it's too soon to consider it a concrete theory, but I think it's worth pursuing, don't you?"

Polly plucked her bag off the back of her chair and slid it up her arm. "Since we don't have a lot of other ideas, I'd say yes."

Glancing at the clock on the wall, Harriet grabbed her bag too. "I didn't realize what time it is. Mike will have our heads."

"Mike is fine. I checked in with him before we stopped here." Polly fell into step with Harriet as they made their way to the door. "He's a good bloke."

"He's the one truly good thing that's come out of the last week or so, for sure," Harriet said, leading the way to her car.

Polly stopped beside the Land Rover to scowl at Harriet. "You take that back."

"Why?" Harriet pulled her door open. "Mike has proven to be a very good hire. He's already done nearly everything on a list I expected to take him a month. He was there for me with the gallery break-in, and again when Princess was taken. And now he's looking after our last boarder so we could go see Cindy."

"It's not the part about him that I'm protesting," Polly said, climbing into the Land Rover and buckling her seat belt. "It's your claim that he's the only good thing."

Sticking the key into the ignition, Harriet flashed a smile at Polly. "You're right. I'm sorry. Your presence and your support throughout all of this have been nothing short of a blessing."

"And?"

Harriet searched her memory as the engine roared to life. "And you made it so I could sleep the night after the break-in by fielding all our after-hours calls. To say nothing of that lovely banoffee pie."

"That's not what I'm talking about."

Harriet backed out of their parking spot. "It appears I'm missing something you've done, and I'm sorry about that. Can we chalk it up to my brain being a bit frazzled?"

"It's not me I'm waiting for you to appreciate. Although I certainly enjoyed hearing all your kind words."

"You deserve them." Harriet pulled onto the road. "Hey, I can scour the living room for those offers myself. I don't need you for that. So how about I drop you off at home rather than drag you back to the clinic? It's not like we have any appointments between now and closing."

"That sounds good. I want you to remember that lots of good things happened this week, even with all the bad."

"*Lots?*" Harriet echoed with a laugh. "I don't know if I agree with that."

"It's true," Polly said stubbornly.

Harriet parked in front of the house Polly shared with her parents. "Well, don't keep me in suspense. I'm dealing with enough mysteries right now."

Polly gave her a knowing smile. "You had that nice visit from Pastor Will the other night."

"You're totally right. I forgot all about that," Harriet said.

"Maxwell's wheels are no longer squeaking," Polly added.

Harriet smiled at her friend. "That's also true."

"You have a friend for life in Murphy."

She felt her smile fall away. "He reminds me of what happened to Princess."

Polly opened her door. "And that's okay, as long as you focus on the good stuff too."

"Good point. Blessings in the storm. All of you."

Polly stepped out of the car. "And you can't forget the best thing of all to happen this week."

"What's that?" Harriet asked.

"Hearing Doc Bailey's voice again."

As she watched Polly make her way to the door, Harriet knew that her friend was absolutely right.

CHAPTER SEVENTEEN

There was no mistaking the irritation on Charlie's face as Harriet moved everything from the end table to the couch yet again.

"I know, I know. I'm disturbing your sacred beauty sleep," Harriet said to her. "My apologies."

Charlie flipped her head upside down and covered her face with a paw as Murphy trotted into the living room, Maxwell right behind him.

"Hey, guys, are you here to help me?" Harriet turned back to the now-clear table. "I know I left those offers here."

She crossed to the table's twin on the other side of the couch and quickly unloaded its stack of books, television remote, and notepad and pen onto the last empty cushion.

Charlie raised her head, glared at Harriet, and jumped down to the floor.

"I'm sorry, Charlie. Truly. But I need to find something I know I left on this table. Or the other one. Or *somewhere*."

She flopped onto the spot vacated by Charlie and stared up at the ceiling, mentally replaying the night she'd read the offers. She'd eaten dinner on the couch while listening to one of her grandfather's tapes. She'd prayed for Nessie's safety and Cindy's peace of mind. She'd washed the dishes she'd used and tidied up the kitchen.

Then she'd started back into the living room to watch TV when she'd noticed the envelopes Ida had given her. She opened them on the couch, read them, shook her head at the notion people would pay such amounts for a painting, and then balled them up, knowing she wouldn't sell that precious piece. Ever. Then she'd changed her mind about throwing them away and set them aside to show Aunt Jinny.

"Maybe the housekeeper of my dreams threw them away by accident." She had to laugh, and Murphy wagged his tail at the sound. "You boys want to go for a walk around the garden before we call it a night?"

Murphy's tail wagged harder, and Maxwell yipped.

"Good." She stood, grabbed Murphy's leash and a flashlight, and opened the French door. "I could use a little fresh air too. And then I believe a visit with Grandad is in order."

Harriet shut off her bedside alarm and rolled onto her back, the first vestiges of morning peeking around her bedroom shade. Charlie gave an indignant meow at the movement.

"Sorry to disturb you, Your Majesty," she murmured.

Charlie stretched her front paws across the blanket and peered over the edge of the bed at Maxwell with more than a hint of superiority.

Swinging her legs over the side of the bed, Harriet sat up and smiled down at the drowsy dachshund. He and Murphy got along well, but Harriet had moved Maxwell's bed into her room for the night to be on the safe side. "Don't mind her, buddy. You're going to get a special treat for breakfast," Harriet said around a yawn.

"Because you recognize that this was a special occasion and are grateful for what you get, aren't you?"

She bent over, rubbed Maxwell beneath his chin, and then stood, the joy she'd fallen asleep with resurfacing as a smile she felt deep inside her soul. Even though it had been a short night—it was after one when she'd finally shut everything down—it had been a good night, a needed night. Listening to her grandfather talk about his love of animals and the way they spoke to his heart had helped lift her spirits. Yes, bad things had happened the past week—things that needed to be figured out and fixed. But she was confident she and Polly were on the right track.

She checked the clock on her nightstand and calculated how much time she had to get her morning to-do list done before Polly arrived for their abbreviated Saturday hours. She had to walk Murphy and make sure he was ready to go home, get breakfast for the animals as well as herself, and shower.

She stood, stretched, picked up Maxwell from his temporarily relocated bed, and followed Charlie down the stairs. At the bottom, she fastened the dachshund into his wheeled prosthesis then shivered. "Wow. It's chilly in here, isn't it?" She rubbed her arms briskly as she called toward the living room, "Murphy? Want some breakfast?"

She listened for the jingle of his collar as he vacated whatever comfy spot he'd found for himself, but there was nothing.

"Murphy?" she called again, but still there was no response.

"Did he fall asleep in one of the other rooms upstairs?" she asked Maxwell. She went back to the stairs and called, "Murphy? Come on, boy. It's the big day. You're getting picked up by your family this morning."

She waited, listening, and then started toward the kitchen and the living room. "Maxwell, why is it so cold in here?"

Her gaze fell on the slightly ajar back door.

"Oh no. No, no, no." She took off at a run, her heart jackhammering against the walls of her chest as her mind ran over the previous evening.

Murphy's evening walk, when she'd thrown his favorite glow-in-the-dark tennis ball until the ringing of her phone called them inside.

The sound of the back door closing behind them with the push of her hand.

Polly's empathetic sigh in her ear when she admitted her failure at finding the painting offers.

Listening to her grandfather's tapes until she felt her eyes drifting shut, settling Murphy on his blankets in the living room, gathering Maxwell and his bed, and taking him and Charlie up the stairs to her bedroom.

The click of her lamp as she shut it off for the night.

"I didn't lock the door," she cried as she dashed out into the garden. "Murphy!" she shouted at the top of her lungs. "Come here, boy!"

She checked the barn, where there was no sign of the Labrador, then made a beeline for the gallery. She circled the outbuildings and the clinic, checked the parking area, and then ran back to the house.

But there was no denying it. Murphy was gone.

CHAPTER EIGHTEEN

Harriet accepted the mug of hot chocolate from Aunt Jinny and tried to rally a smile, but it was impossible. She stared at the dollop of whipped cream she'd heard Polly insist upon and replayed the images she'd been picturing in her mind's eye for hours.

"I keep seeing Grandad's face in my head," she whispered. "Except that instead of his ever-ready smile, I see confusion and sadness."

Aunt Jinny dropped onto the couch beside Harriet. "I'm sure he'd be as confused as we are. I don't know how he couldn't be. And the sadness? That makes sense too. You got your love of animals from him."

"Mostly, though, I see disappointment in his eyes." Harriet heard the tremble in her voice but was powerless to make it stop. "Disappointment in me."

"Why on earth would you say that? He loved you, Harriet."

"I know he did. But I also know he trusted me to do right by the clinic. By his reputation."

Aunt Jinny met her gaze squarely. "You closed the door behind you after Murphy's walk, right?"

"I did."

"Well, Murphy didn't let himself out."

"I know that. But I didn't lock it like I should have."

"You are hardly at fault for someone else deciding to take advantage of an unlocked door. Beating yourself up over it isn't going to solve anything."

Lifting her fingers to her cheeks, Harriet wiped at the tears she couldn't blink away fast enough. "I need to call Murphy's family, but I don't know if I can."

"You can, and you will. The longer you wait, the worse it will be. And after you do, you'll get back to work."

Harriet sniffled. "There is no work to get back to, Aunt Jinny. No one wants to trust their pet to a failed veterinarian like me."

"Murphy was stolen by a thief. That's not a failure on your part."

"Out of my home—a home I forgot to lock up despite everything that's happened this past week," Harriet said. "Would *you* trust your pet to someone who did that? Because I wouldn't."

Before her aunt could respond, Harriet pushed off the couch and crossed into the kitchen where Polly sat on the floor with Maxwell and Charlie. "It's time to call Murphy's owners. I can't delay this any longer, no matter how much I wish I could."

Polly followed Harriet into the clinic. "I can make the call if you'd like, boss. You've been through enough this morning."

"No. I made this mess. I'll make the call." She stepped into her office and started to close the door but stopped long enough to meet her friend's worry-filled eyes. "Say a prayer for me, okay?"

"I've been saying them all morning."

Harriet drew in a breath, held it, and then closed the door between them, her heart aching. "I'm sorry, Murphy. I truly, truly am," she whispered as she crossed to her desk and the telephone number she knew waited on top for this very moment.

It took three tries before she had the numbers typed in correctly. And it took a couple deep breaths before she pressed the green button to actually put the call through. But the moment she heard the happy greeting on the other end of the line, she wished the floor would open and swallow her whole.

"We're on our way, Dr. Bailey. We're about two hours out, and as wonderful as our holiday was, there's not a person in this car who isn't excited to see our boy."

Harriet's throat constricted, and she coughed to clear it enough that she could force the words out. "I—I have some bad news, I'm afraid."

Twenty minutes later, with the cries of Murphy's owners still ringing in her ears, Harriet stepped out of her office to find Polly waiting, concern front and center on her friend's face.

"You okay?"

Harriet laced her hands behind her head and shook her head, unable to speak.

"Come sit down." Polly guided Harriet into the waiting area and sat beside her. "We need to talk."

Something about Polly's voice stirred an immediate groan from Harriet's soul. "What other awful thing has happened?"

"I hesitate to call someone's offer to help an awful thing, but I think it means we're back to square one. At least as far as Nessie and the painting are concerned."

Harriet stared at her friend, unable to process, unable to comment because of the fog in her mind.

"Dale Renner stopped by while you were on the phone."

She shot out of her chair. "And? Did he bring Nessie? Wait. What you said about being back at square one. It's not him, is it?"

"I'm afraid not."

"And we know this how?" Harriet asked.

"Because he came by to let us know he read the report on Scout, verified it with a friend of a friend who's a vet, and deleted his bad reviews," Polly said.

Harriet sat back down, absorbing what she'd heard.

"He also said he's organizing a group of friends to search for Nessie, Princess, and now Murphy. Because—get this—he wants to find the person who could steal people's pets, and escort them to jail himself."

"And you could tell he meant it?" she asked.

Polly's nod was not unexpected, but it still smarted.

"I didn't really want it to be him," Harriet said. "But if we'd been right, it would have meant an end to at least part of this insanity, if not all of it. But now, not only is it *not* him, but Murphy has been stolen as well."

Polly wordlessly laid a comforting hand on her arm.

Harriet rested her chin on her hand. "I'd give just about anything to have Grandad here right now. He'd know what to do."

"He might not be able to tell you what to do, but he can help you think about something else for a little while."

Harriet didn't mean to laugh at the absurdity of Polly's words, but she couldn't help it. "I'm pretty sure that's not possible."

"I think it's worth a try, don't you?" Polly suggested.

"It sounds like you have an idea to prove me wrong."

"It's your aunt's idea, actually. She brought it up to me while you were on the phone with Murphy's owner."

"There's no work to be done here today. I already told her that," Harriet said, kneading at her temples.

Polly stood and tugged her to her feet. "She said you should sit down with Ida and figure out how to implement the idea of the gallery audio tour."

Harriet started to argue, to remind Polly of everything going on that would make that difficult, but then the wisdom of the suggestion sank in. "I could use a little more Grandad time. And we could certainly use a new attraction to bring people into the gallery."

Polly started toward the doorway that led to the house. "I'm sure Jinny would be happy to sit at the desk in the gallery for a little while so Ida can come here and work with you on it."

"No." Harriet locked the clinic door and caught up with Polly. "I think we could all use a little time with him right about now, don't you?"

CHAPTER NINETEEN

Armed with the tape recorder in one hand and a tote bag of tapes over her shoulder, Harriet let her grandfather lead a tour around the gallery with his rich voice, his words and stories bringing new life to his work, so familiar to all of them.

They heard about the sweet calf who'd inspired his first-ever animal painting, *The First Unsteady Steps to Greatness*. They heard about Bertha the cockapoo, Marigold the golden retriever, Prince the Shetland pony, and so many more. As Harriet had expected, nothing compared to hearing her grandfather speak about his paintings in his own words while admiring the work itself.

"Oh, Imogen," Aunt Jinny said, pressing her hands to her cheeks as she, Polly, and Ida stopped in front of the next painting. "This has always been one of my favorites of the paintings he didn't give away or sell."

Harriet looked at the Ragdoll cat. "I haven't listened to the tape about Imogen yet." She loaded the tape labeled with the cat's name into the machine, and her grandfather's voice filled the air once more.

"Ragdolls like Imogen are very puppy-like in the way they follow their owners around," he said, his voice as clear as if he were in the room with them. "They also seem to be able to sense their owner's emotions, making them loyal, comforting companions."

Harriet matched the smile she heard in her grandfather's voice as he continued. "Imogen was no exception. She loved her family fiercely, and they loved her just as fiercely in return."

"I remember that cat," Aunt Jinny said. "Dad always blocked off extra time for her appointments because he loved that she'd play fetch with him."

Harriet took in the cat's cream-colored body, its brown-tipped ears and nose, its large blue eyes, and the inverted V-shape on its forehead—all details of the Ragdoll breed she knew from veterinarian school—as her grandfather's voice walked them through the image of Imogen he'd chosen to capture with his paintbrush.

"Unlike most other breeds of cats, Ragdolls enjoy water. They like playing with it, exploring it, and even bathing in it. Which is why, when Imogen came in to see me, I blocked out enough time for a quick bath. Not because she was dirty, mind you, but because I found it fun. I'd fill up a metal wash bucket to the appropriate water level, set her inside, and let her play with the same little yellow duck my granddaughter, Harriet, played with as a toddler when she came for a visit. The image perfectly captures Imogen's playful personality and is also a subtle nod to my beloved Harriet."

Harriet gasped as her eyes filled. "I played with that same duck? He put that in there for me?"

Laughing, Aunt Jinny reached over and paused the recording. "Apparently."

"People always love Imogen when they come into the gallery," Ida said. "They find it funny to see a cat in a bucket of water, playing with a rubber duck. As if it could never happen outside a painting."

Harriet took in every inch of the artwork she'd always loved yet now felt as if she were seeing for the very first time. "But it did. As did every scene with every animal he painted."

"A statement I repeat in here at least a dozen times a day." Ida stepped to the left for a different view of Imogen's painting. "You can actually feel her joy, can't you? Harold perfectly captured the emotion in the brightness of her eyes. They almost seem to glow."

Harriet continued the tape.

"It was always special when Imogen came to the clinic for a checkup. She was playful and fun. But perhaps what captured me most about her was the way she made me think about my cherished wife, Helen."

Aunt Jinny beamed. "I can't wait to hear this."

"Before you go thinking I'm being disrespectful, comparing my late wife and the mother of my children to a cat, hear me out. Imogen was loyal and true to her family, like my Helen. She was curious and fun, like my Helen. She was the prettiest cat I'd ever seen, as my Helen was the prettiest woman I'd ever seen. And when I'd lean down to greet Imogen, she'd press her forehead to mine and just hold it there, something my Helen did with me every day we were together on this earth."

Feeling a lump rise in her throat, Harriet took Aunt Jinny's hand.

"I thought about painting that moment when Imogen would press her forehead to mine instead of the one of her in the wash bucket. But then I would have had to paint myself, and I wanted it to be about her, not me."

Harriet waited a few seconds to see if he would speak again, but when he didn't, she stopped the recording and pulled in a deep breath. "Wow," she said. "Grandad really worked his love into everything he did, didn't he? With the tributes to Gran and me in this painting, where I never would have expected them, I have to wonder how many of his other paintings contain touches for someone he cared about."

"Wow is right." Polly lifted her hand to her cheek and wiped away a tear.

Harriet peeked over at her aunt. "You okay, Aunt Jinny?"

"I am," Aunt Jinny said. "That was beautiful."

"It really was. I still wish I could have met Gran." Unfortunately, her grandmother had passed before Harriet was born.

"I wish you could have too, Harriet." Aunt Jinny wiped her eyes and straightened. "I'm so glad you want to make this an experience for all the gallery's visitors. How do you plan to do it?"

"Ida reported that after Nessie's disappearance, we had a massive influx of donations," Harriet explained. "I want to use the extra funds to digitize these tapes into audio files, which we'll store online. Visitors will be able to scan a code with their phones when they arrive, and that will take them to the files. Then they'll be able to select the file of the painting they want to hear about as they move around the gallery. It should be fairly simple and relatively inexpensive for us to set up. It will also enrich our visitors' experience and give people who've already been here a new reason to come back."

Aunt Jinny squeezed her hand, pride shining in her eyes. "That's wonderful, Harriet."

Silence settled over the group as they took a few more moments to admire Imogen, each lost in her own thoughts. Eventually, though, they moved along as a group—and stopped.

"I wish Van and the others would hurry up and find Nessie's painting," Polly said, gazing at the vacant spot on the wall.

Harriet willed herself to stay positive. "He's trying. I know he is. We have to give him and the rest of the police force time to do their job."

"Is it okay if we keep listening though?" Ida asked. "I'd love to hear Doc Bailey's words about the Nessie painting."

Harriet riffled through the tapes but couldn't find the one Grandad had made about Nessie. "I'm sorry, Ida," she said. "I must have left that in the house. We can listen to this one about how he started painting though." Harriet replaced the tape on Imogen with the one marked MY STORY. Her grandfather's voice filled the room once again with the words she'd heard so many times she was starting to memorize them.

"My dear wife, Helen, was a questioner. Didn't matter whether she knew you for years or had just met you at the market. She said asking questions and listening to the answers was how families grew closer and strangers became friends. She asked me to make this tape, insisting that someday someone would want my story too. This is what led me to painting. It's not all that exciting, really, but my Helen said it mattered, and I learned early on not to argue with her. So this is for the woman I still feel in my heart every single day."

Aunt Jinny slanted a smile at Harriet. "I love hearing him talk about that because it's so true. Mum said that to him all the time. To your dad and me too."

Harriet wrapped her arm around her aunt's shoulders and remained silent as her grandfather continued his story.

"I'm not sure whether people realize it, but so many of the animals I've treated over the years have become like family to me. I'm happy to see them when they come in for a checkup, and I worry when they come to me during an illness. Each one has a personality of their own. Some let me see it the moment I first lay eyes on them. Others make me work for it, revealing various bits and pieces over time."

Harriet watched the other women listen to the words, drinking in their pleasure as her grandfather's voice continued, his words, his tone, and his passion clearly giving each of them the lift they needed.

"From the timid hamster who prefers to eat when no one is watching to the dog who faithfully cared for a litter of orphaned kittens until they were old enough to thrive on their own, each and every animal that has come through my door has left an indelible impression on my soul. I've often found my words inadequate in describing those impressions. Yet when I put paint to canvas, that changes. Instead of trying to put what I see into words that never seem to do an animal justice, I've found that I can *show* what I see. That, my dear Helen, is the story behind my animal paintings."

Ida sucked in a breath. "Oh, this would be perfect for the start of an audio tour."

"I think so too," Harriet agreed. "I could listen to that one again and again, couldn't you?"

About thirty seconds into Ida's and Aunt Jinny's excited chatter about how they could advertise the audio tour, a sound like that of a chair scraping against a floor emerged from the tape recorder, which Harriet had left on.

Polly clapped her hands. "Wait! It's still going."

Harriet hadn't realized there was more on the tape, as she'd always stopped it during the long silence. Her jaw dropped as she heard her grandad's voice again.

"Now I know I'm not supposed to have favorites, but I could go on and on about Nessie. I remember the first day I met her like it was yesterday. I was sitting at my desk, working on a file, when Felix burst through my door. I remember wondering what I'd done that time. Were my fen violets blooming better than his? Had he intended to buy the exact pair of loafers I'd gotten in town the previous day? Had I taken a breath of the air he wanted to breathe? I didn't know, but I figured any or all of that was possible."

Harriet heard weariness in Grandad's voice. But it vanished at his next words.

"Instead, Felix came to tell me about a days-old kitten he had spotted in a pile of rocks. He suspected she was stuck, and he couldn't help her on account of being severely allergic to cats. So I jumped up, grabbed some things I thought might prove helpful, and ran down there."

Even though Harriet knew the story, she found herself caught up in the suspense and excitement of her grandfather's telling.

"I'll never forget seeing her little face peering out from between the rocks. Her fear, confusion, and loneliness. They were all the same things I'd felt when I lost my Helen. Naturally, I would have done anything to help any animal in that situation, but there was something different about Nessie, something that reached into my chest and grabbed my heart."

Harriet knew what he meant. She'd had similar experiences herself.

"A passerby captured her rescue with his camera and shared the photos with the local paper. For weeks after that story ran, people stopped me in the store or on the road to ask about Nessie and to thank me for rescuing her."

Aunt Jinny smiled. "I remember that. They called him a hero, and they were right."

"As much as I enjoyed caring for her," Grandad continued, "I always suspected that she was meant for someone else. So, when the time was right, I gave her to my late friend's daughter, a woman who felt all of the things Nessie did when she was stuck between those rocks."

"Cindy," Polly said beneath her breath.

"And as I'll never forget the flash of hope I saw in Nessie's eyes when I set about freeing her from those rocks that day, I'll never forget the instant love in her new mum's eyes the moment I brought the two of them together."

Harriet realized she was beaming at the sweet tale.

Grandad cleared his throat. "That's what animals do for those willing to love them. They give us hope and new purpose. They remind us to love and to be loved in the way our Lord loves us— unconditionally and without fail."

This time, Harriet let the tape play all the way to the end, but there was no more on it. "That was beautiful," she whispered.

"I'm so glad you found these tapes, Harriet." Aunt Jinny reached into her pocket, extracted a tissue, and blew her nose. "What a gift they are."

Harriet nodded. "They are, indeed. If not for Charlie and her attic snooping, years could have gone by before I realized they were up there."

Ida held a finger to her lips. "Wait. Do you hear that?"

Polly cocked her head. "Hear what?"

"Listen."

They waited through a few moments of silence until Ida lowered her hand. "Okay, don't mind me. It must have been my imagination."

"No, I hear it too," Aunt Jinny said.

Crossing to Ida's desk, Harriet set down the recorder and tapes. She was halfway to the nearest window to peer out for the source of the sound when the front door swung open and a familiar pair walked in.

"Hi, Harriet," Candace sang out. "We were hoping we'd find you in here. We got a call from the neighbor of someone whose dog was stolen from your home last night. What can you tell us about that?"

Harriet tried to cling to the calm she'd managed to cultivate over the past two hours, but it slipped away.

Polly came forward. "We don't have anything to share beyond whatever you've heard."

Candace zeroed in on her. "Did they break a window to get inside? Was anything else taken?"

Polly lifted her chin. "No."

"No jewelry or money? Nothing else, just the dog?"

Harriet stared at Candace. "Are those actual questions, or are you fishing for answers you already know?"

Candace fiddled with her sleeves. "Did you find a note?"

"No."

"Are you sure you didn't miss one?" Doug asked.

Harriet clenched her jaw. "There was no note."

Candace slumped.

"I'm sorry, does that tidbit disappoint you somehow?" Harriet demanded.

"No, it intrigues me."

"Why is that?" Harriet prodded.

"Two of the four crimes perpetrated here had notes, but the other two didn't."

"Nessie wasn't taken from my home," Harriet reminded her. "She was taken from her own."

Candace surveyed the gallery before her gaze came back to Harriet. "But she was connected enough to this place that her abductor slid a note under your clinic's door."

Doug shook his head. "The viewers don't need notes, Candace. They need the best story we can give them. And the suits want you to do more of what you've been doing since this whole thing started."

Candace squared her shoulders. "What Doug is saying is that my work this past week has been a bit of a ratings bonanza for the station. People are practically glued to their television screens waiting for the next installment of your saga."

"Which means we should head back outside and get to work," Doug said. "We play it right, Candace, and you're moving on to your dream spot as a weekend anchor."

"Enough!" Aunt Jinny stepped to Harriet's side and laid a hand on her shoulder. "This isn't about either of your careers. This is about reuniting beloved pets with their grieving owners."

"Aunt Jinny, it's okay. I can handle this."

Candace pointed at Aunt Jinny. "I've done a little research on you since the other evening. You're Dr. Harold Bailey's daughter, yes?"

"I am."

Candace glanced at Doug, who lifted his camera. "As Dr. Harold Bailey's daughter, were you upset when Cobble Hill Farm went to your niece and not you?"

"If you took the time to get to know my niece as a person rather than as simply a story, you wouldn't even ask that question," Aunt Jinny replied. "But since you did, I'll say this. I knew my father's plans for both the farm and his clinic, and I was in perfect agreement. Anything else?"

"Actually, yes." Candace signaled for Doug to keep rolling. "If your father were alive to see everything that's been happening around Cobble Hill Farm the past week, what do you think he'd say?"

Harriet braced herself. Candace obviously meant to twist Aunt Jinny's answer, whatever it was, to make it sound as if Harriet was letting Grandad down, betraying his legacy.

Aunt Jinny eyed the reporter. "To you?"

"Sure."

Aunt Jinny grinned. "I think he'd say, 'No comment.'"

Polly and Ida laughed as Doug lowered his camera to his side.

Aunt Jinny turned to Harriet, her expression softening. "To you, Grandad would take this moment to remind you of one of his favorite Bible verses. Joshua 1:9."

Harriet knew it by heart. "Be strong and courageous. Do not be afraid; do not be discouraged, for the Lord your God will be with you wherever you go."

Aunty Jinny squeezed Harriet's hand. "Hold that close to your heart, and you'll get through all of this. For now, I've got to run, dear. Keep your head up. You're doing right by Dad, and I never want you to doubt that. Try to get some sleep tonight, okay?"

"I'll do my best." She returned her aunt's wave and then turned her attention back to the reporter on the gallery's doorstep. "I'm sorry if she came across a little harsh, but we've been through a lot lately. I know you're just trying to do your job, so I'll answer the question about my grandfather if you'll answer one question for me."

Candace pointed at Doug, waited for him to position the camera on his shoulder, and then held up her hand to delay filming. "Ask away."

"How badly do you want this promotion to weekend anchor?"

Doug laughed. "I can answer that. It's all she's talked about for the past year. 'I want to be an anchor, Doug. I have to be an anchor, Doug. I can do it every bit as well as Giles, and I can do it without putting viewers to sleep, Doug. If I have to drive around in this van for another day, I'm going to scream, Doug.'"

"I'm not that bad," Candace protested.

Doug made a face. "You want to switch places with me for a day?"

Candace's face flushed red. "I'm sorry. I didn't realize—"

"It's fine. We all have aspirations." Doug checked his watch and then jerked his chin toward the door. "I'll meet you in the van. I should call my wife and tell her it'll be another late night."

Candace watched her coworker disappear through the door and then faced the remaining women. "It seems I'm learning a lot of things this week, mostly about myself."

"Is he wrong?" Harriet asked.

Candace tucked a stray lock of hair behind her ear. "That I want this promotion? No. I want it very much. But I do hate that it looks as if it's going to happen at your expense."

It was not the answer Harriet had expected.

If the look on Polly's face was any indication, she felt the same way.

"That surprises me," Harriet admitted.

"It surprises me too. But it's something that's been hovering at the edges of my awareness. I didn't fully realize it until I pulled the tape of you on the bench with your aunt the other day. I knew that was good stuff when Doug and I came around the corner and heard it. But since I took the time to watch it alone at the station, to really listen to it for what it was, I've found myself thinking differently."

"How?"

"From what I've been able to gather this past week talking to folks here in White Church Bay, you gave up your life in the States and moved here to carry on your grandfather's work. I can relate to that. My grandfather was a well-known journalist where I grew up, and I'm always trying to make him proud."

Harriet gave her a small smile. "I know that feeling well."

Candace met her eyes. "But I don't want to achieve my goal at the expense of someone who's trying to do the same thing I am. I'd rather make it because I deliver the happy ending."

Harriet held out her hand. "Candace Moore, I think you and I finally understand each other."

CHAPTER TWENTY

"Harriet, you're here!" Hefting her medical bag, Harriet smiled at the woman who'd opened the door. "You did say eight, right?"

"I did, but you've been dealing with a lot since we agreed to that, and I guess I figured your mind would be elsewhere."

Harriet willed her smile to remain in place even as her thoughts started down a road she was desperate to detour from, if only for a little while. "I think time with Wilson is exactly what this doctor orders."

"I'm glad to hear it." Theresa motioned Harriet inside. "Welcome to our home away from home. I gave my landlord the scoop about the handyman you have working at your compound and his ability to fix screechy doors and broken windows, et cetera, et cetera."

"Is that a term people in the UK use when referring to a big piece of property with a few outbuildings?" Harriet asked as she followed her hostess.

"What? Compound?"

"Yes. You're the second person who's referred to my farm as a compound in the last few days. I took it as a bit of a slight toward me last time, but now I'm wondering if it's just something that's said and I've never really noticed it until now."

"I'm not from here, remember?" Theresa replied. "So I can't say one way or the other. I simply assumed that's how everyone refers to your setup, since you have multiple homes and businesses there. I'm sorry if I offended you."

"You didn't. The word caught me by surprise, that's all."

"I understand." Theresa splayed her hands. "I'd like to think the man who owns this place will inquire about your handyman, but I know he won't. Mr. Littleton doesn't care. He already has my signature on the rental agreement."

Harriet took in the dingy walls and uneven floor but said nothing as Theresa closed the door on the entryway's sole source of natural light.

"And I don't have the time or the desire for even a small claims court at the moment," she went on. "Not with my book and Wilson's continuing difficulties."

Harriet did her best to keep her expression neutral, but it was hard. The place truly was a disaster.

"In the interest of silver linings, I'm thrilled with the story I've come up with, and the words are finally beginning to flow, more or less," Theresa added.

"Polly will be pleased to hear that," Harriet told her. "How is Wilson this—"

She was interrupted by a bark. One she recognized, to her shock.

"Murphy?" Harriet steadied herself against the wall. "He's *here*?"

Theresa clicked her door's lock into place, eyeing Harriet over her shoulder as she did. "Murphy's the dog they talked about on the news last night, right? The one that was taken from your farm?"

"It is. And that barking sounded just like him."

"Nope. That's Wilson being Wilson."

Harriet heard a squeal, followed by a thud, then repeated clicks. She gaped at the author. "What is that?"

"That would be Wilson's latest installment. But wait for it. Now he's going to add those sounds to the end of all his other sounds from this past week. I've started calling it his magnum opus."

Sure enough, a cacophony of sounds—including three clicks, what sounded like an "ow," a slightly higher-pitched bark, a thud, and three clicks again—met Harriet's ears, followed by the same combination that had initially greeted her.

Theresa waited until silence fell then remarked dryly, "I keep telling him he should try it in a minor key, but he's the composer. So I'm sure he knows best."

Harriet widened her gaze back at Theresa. "What on earth?"

"That's what I was hoping to ask you. Welcome to the craziness that is the first hour or so of my day, every day, as of late." Theresa's laugh held signs of strain. "Nuts, right? I mean, when he started with the first part, I wanted to pull my hair out after about the dozenth time. But now, after these latest additions, I find myself desperately wishing I could rewind to the morning when the first few noises were the extent of his battle cry."

"He's added things in stages?" Harriet asked.

Theresa led the way down the hall. "It certainly feels that way. When he does have a new combination, he tries it out a few times by itself. Then he runs through all of them in order, inserting the newest segment at the end, as you heard when you came in."

"Interesting," Harriet mused.

"That's not the word I would choose to sum this up, but you're the professional." At the end of the hallway, Theresa turned in to a room with paneled walls, sloped flooring, and a large window overlooking a single chair on a small screened-in patio. "When he finishes all the repetitions of his latest performance that he thinks are necessary, he goes completely silent, turns his back to me, and starts messing with his feathers again."

Beyond the patio was a small, unkempt yard, featuring a dilapidated shed in the far-left corner, weed-infested grass, and a broken split-rail fence.

Wilson repeated all the sounds, in the same order from what Harriet could tell.

Harriet spotted Wilson's cage in the corner of the room and made her way to it. "And he didn't make these sounds before you moved to White Church Bay?"

One by one, Wilson squawked out the same sounds in the same order.

Theresa waited until he finished before she answered, leaning against the wall beside his cage. "No. He talked to me normally. He'd tell me it was going to be a 'sunny day,' or that I needed to 'write, write, write.' That sort of thing. It was fun, and occasionally motivational. But these noises are new since we got here, to this awful place." She scanned their surroundings with a grimace.

"I'm so sorry you've gotten that impression," Harriet said. "White Church Bay is really a very special town."

"Oh no, I was talking about this dreadful little cottage. The town and its people have been very welcoming," Theresa assured her.

"I'm glad to hear that." Harriet focused on the bird in front of her. "So you're happy with the story you're writing?"

"Very happy. A lot of it is due to the stories that reporter has been doing on you, and the very real fact that pretty much everyone around me seems to have either a cat or a dog, or both."

"I don't understand," Harriet said. "What does any of that have to do with your next book?"

"I've always known people had a soft spot for animals. But the interest in that woman's stolen cat and the people I'm seeing around town who are here for no other reason than to help find Nessie made me realize that crafting a romance with a backdrop of animals was the way to go. Although it's writing more as a romantic suspense, much to my editor's chagrin. Sometimes I really am a trial to her."

Harriet slowly moved to the side of the cage that afforded the best view of Wilson's face, trying not to spook him. "I'm sure it'll be great. Polly is a huge fan."

"I'm glad someone is," Theresa teased.

Her cheeks warming, Harriet lifted her gaze to Theresa's. "Polly's told me I need to try your books, but with everything that's been happening, I haven't had a chance."

Theresa waved aside Harriet's discomfort. "It's okay if you haven't read my work. I don't take offense. I promise."

"It's just that when I do pick up a book specifically for the purpose of reading for fun, it's usually at the very end of the day," Harriet hurried to explain. "When I'm in bed."

Theresa laughed. "And you wake up in the morning with the same book sitting open on your chest?"

"Pathetic, I know," Harriet said as Wilson turned away from both of them.

"I suspect that's more about putting in long days taking care of everyone's animals than it is about being pathetic."

Harriet watched the bird rock on his perch a few times. "Maybe. But I can't use that rationale as an excuse any longer, that's for sure."

"Meaning?"

"Let's just say the events of the past week have cut down on my time taking care of animals."

Twisting his head to the right, Wilson reached over his shoulder, rooted between his side feathers, and pulled back with a vengeance. Sure enough, a feather fluttered to the bottom of the cage.

Theresa clapped her hands. "Wilson, stop! You'll go bald, you silly bird."

Wilson ignored her.

"And this is part two of our new morning routine," Theresa groused.

Harriet made her way around the cage until she and Theresa were on opposite sides then moved her head around in an attempt to attract the parrot's attention. Wilson's gaze remained downward. "Tell me about his behavior the rest of the day. Specifically, what's changed since you came to White Church Bay."

"He's very quiet and withdrawn, as you can see." Theresa waved at the cage. "He starts with the sounds. Then he falls silent, avoids eye contact, and begins playing with his feathers. Sometimes, he merely pushes at them with his beak, as if he's just grooming himself. But other times he pulls one out, like he did today. It might be less noticeable if he took them from different spots, but he doesn't, as you can see."

Harriet examined the area Wilson clearly favored for plucking. "Which he's done three times so far, right? So not every day since the new sounds started."

"Correct."

"Was anything different on the days he *did* pull out feathers?" Harriet asked.

"You mean beyond his sounds?"

"Yes."

Theresa wandered over to an overstuffed chair covered with books and cleared a spot for herself to sit. "I mean, I'm writing, or trying to write, or trying out various parts of my plot most days. But he's used to that. He likes the change of scenery that gives him."

"How do you do that?"

"I move him to wherever I'm working, usually on his perch so he can roam. But he's been preferring the cage lately, so I haven't even been moving the perch. If I'm making notes here"—Theresa patted her armrests—"or doing research or writing at my desk, I have his cage where it is right now. That way, if he wants to see me, he can. And I can talk to him and try to reassure him, for all the good that's done. If I sit outside on the screened-in porch, he's either out there with me or there by the window where he can see me. If I opt for the latter, I'll talk to him through a baby monitor. The only time he's not with me is if I need to go somewhere to try out a plot point or gather some props for a scene I'm trying to set."

"Have you always moved him around like that?" Harriet asked. "I mean, with past books you've written?"

"Yes. He's so used to it that he makes a fuss if I try to leave him behind. At least, he used to."

"Is this the first time you've taken up residency somewhere new to write?"

"Since I've had Wilson, yes."

Harriet lowered herself to eye level with the parrot. "Wilson, it's okay," she told him in a quiet, steady voice. "You're safe. No one is going to hurt you."

He glanced up, met her eyes, and then dropped his attention back to the floor of his cage.

"Is he going to be okay, Harriet?" Theresa asked.

"I'm not sure yet, but he actually made eye contact. That's progress, I believe," Harriet replied. "Has anything about your routine changed, other than the venue?"

Theresa stood, wandered over to the window, and blew out a breath. "I'll admit that it took me longer to settle on a plot than is normally the case for me. Every stage of my usual process has taken longer this time. But I'm actually doing some writing now, so that's something."

"I'm pretty sure I just heard Polly cheer from wherever she is at this particular moment." Harriet gave a soft laugh and was delighted when Wilson gave her another glance. "Maybe, in addition to the move, he picked up on whatever stress you may have been feeling when the plot was taking longer to reveal itself to you."

Theresa made her way back to the far side of the cage. "I suppose that's possible. I mean, I did a lot of pacing before my plot finally came together. A looming deadline with absolutely no ideas has a way of inciting that. Even so, I've been in a much better place these last few days. But Wilson is still rocking, making strange noises, and plucking his feathers out."

"He plucked out his first feathers last Saturday, right?" Harriet asked.

"Yes, I believe that's right. But let me check." Theresa hurried to her desk and grabbed a spiral-bound planner. She flipped it open then thumbed through it until she found what she wanted. "Here it is. I noted it the first morning I brought him in to see you. Which was also the same morning he started with the random sounds."

Harriet filed the information away in her thoughts as Wilson looked up at her again. This time, though, he kept looking at her. "What are you trying to tell us, sweet boy?" Harriet whispered to him. "We're listening."

Theresa hummed over her planner. "That's interesting. I can't believe I didn't notice it before."

"What's interesting?" Harriet asked, careful to maintain the soothing quality of her voice and the softness in her face as Wilson continued to watch her.

"The next time he plucked his feathers was the same day he added to his monologue."

Harriet couldn't help but smile at the writer's word choice. "Oh?"

"I wrote down that I called you about it. And then he plucked again today, right in front of you," Theresa said. "After another round of new sounds. Weird, right? It can't be a coincidence."

"He's definitely trying to tell us something. We're listening, Wilson," Harriet said again.

Wilson rocked and then slowly faced Theresa.

"Phew. He's done."

Harriet straightened up for an uninhibited view of the woman on the other side of the room. "How do you know?" she asked.

"After the sounds, he avoids me and rocks. Then he either plays with his feathers or pulls them out. Then he stares at the floor of his cage. Eventually, he turns back to where he can see me, and he's the Wilson I know for the rest of the day, although he's quieter than usual."

Harriet took in the bird once again, his body language more relaxed than it had been. "You're right. He's calmer now."

"Any thoughts?" Theresa asked.

"I'm still confident he's trying to tell us something."

"Do you think he's sick?"

"My instincts say no. But I'm going to keep an eye on him and continue to do research on African grays." Harriet checked the time and backed away from the cage. "Call me if he plucks again. And keep doing what you're doing with the notes on when he does what. It's a good idea."

"I will. Thank you for coming over," Theresa said. "How are you holding up with everything that's going on?"

Harriet felt as if the air rushed out of her lungs. Logically, she knew there was nothing else she could do for Wilson at the moment, but suddenly she felt he was simply one more animal she was letting down. "I don't know. I'm trying not to think about it, but I also think about it all the time."

"That's obvious by the way you reacted to Wilson's sounds when you walked in this morning."

Shrugging, Harriet tried hard to make her lips curve upward in a smile, but she knew her effort came off strained at best. "Clearly, I have Murphy on my thoughts. Along with Nessie and Princess."

"I can imagine. It seems every night on the local news, there's another development," Theresa observed.

"Because there is."

"What are you doing with your boarders now?" Theresa asked.

Harriet swallowed. "I don't have any boarders left."

Theresa laid her hand on Harriet's forearm. "I'm sure you'll get some soon."

"Would you leave a pet with me after everything that's happened?" Harriet asked, her voice thick with emotion she could no longer keep at bay.

"I would."

She raised her eyebrows in disbelief. "Really?"

"After the kindness and compassion you've shown Wilson, absolutely."

"Thank you."

"Of course," Theresa said. "Hey, I also noticed that all but one of those one-star reviews have suddenly disappeared. Surely that's a good sign?"

Harriet drew back. "They didn't all go away?"

"No, there's still one, I'm afraid. But maybe, if I get a moment between writing sessions today, I'll post a five-star review that will offset the one posted by 'Gof,' whoever that is."

Harriet closed her eyes for a moment. "Gof?"

"Do you know who that is?" Theresa asked.

"I thought I did. But the fact that it's still up tells me I was wrong."

"Well, it doesn't matter. If I was checking reviews for something as important as a vet, I'd want to read people's thoughts and feedback. I wouldn't just look at stars, and that post doesn't have any comments. They merely clicked the one-star rating and posted it."

Harriet ran her fingers along the top of Wilson's cage. "Do you think everyone is like you?"

"No. But I'm going to write a review people won't soon forget."

"Thank you. With how many people are probably researching me online because of the news, it can't hurt for them to see some good stuff too."

"We can hope," Theresa said.

Harriet tapped her watch. "Anyway, I really should get going. I don't want to be late for church. Or a chance at one of Doreen Danby's famous scones."

"I totally understand. Oh!" Theresa suddenly snatched a notebook and pen from her writing station and jotted something down. When she finished, she gave Harriet a rueful smile. "Sorry. Things have a way of coming to me at the weirdest times. I've found that if I don't make a note of it in the moment, I risk forgetting it."

"I'm that way with my grocery list."

"You and me both." Theresa escorted her to the door. "Since Wilson seems to be having a particularly rough day, I'm going to stay home with him this morning. But thank you for checking in on him, Harriet. It really means a lot."

Harriet told her goodbye and left, grateful that at least one person still believed in her competence at her job.

CHAPTER TWENTY-ONE

Harriet sat alone in the pew.

Her fellow churchgoers had left a while before. As they did every Sunday, they'd gotten up after the final hymn and made their way to the back of the church, greeting one another and Pastor Will. The lucky ones even secured one of Doreen Danby's famous scones.

It was what she'd assumed she would do too.

When she'd walked through the door more than an hour earlier, she'd felt deeply alone. Yet, as the service began and Will preached, she'd felt all of that slip away until it was just her and God.

Yes, Nessie was still missing. As was the painting, and Harriet's two boarders. While all but one of the bad reviews had been taken down, the fact that they'd been there at all certainly didn't help the clinic's current situation.

But there, in God's house, surrounded by His Word, she didn't feel quite so alone.

"Harriet?"

Harriet jumped and spun toward the center aisle. "Will! I—I'm sorry. I know you probably want to head out. I was just soaking in the peace."

"No, please." He set his hand gently on her shoulder. "I was hoping we'd get a chance to talk this morning. May I join you?"

"Of course." She slid down to make room for him and smiled as he handed her a scone on a napkin. "This is for me?"

"It is."

"Thank you."

He twisted to face her. "How are you holding up?"

She had broken off a piece of scone but set it back on the napkin instead of putting it in her mouth. "Until I sat down in here, not as well as I'd like. Which is why I'm still here instead of heading home like everyone else. I don't want to leave His presence."

"He's with you no matter where you are. You know that."

"I do." She gazed at the cross on the wall behind the altar. "I'm sure you've seen the news like everyone else clearly has. Everything feels like too much. And I want to fix it all, but I don't know how—or even if I can."

"I haven't seen the news. I'd rather hear about it from you, anyway. While you eat that scone."

"Will you share it with me?" she asked.

"I'd be delighted."

At his answering smile, she broke the scone in two and handed him the bigger piece. He took a bite. After she followed suit, he said, "Catch me up on everything that's happened since I stopped by your house."

"Thank you for that, by the way. I enjoyed the visit."

He smiled again. "As did I."

She took another bite of the pastry and found that it nourished her almost as much as the presence of the man beside her, to say nothing of their surroundings. "If I remember correctly, you stopped by after the gallery was broken into and my grandfather's painting was stolen."

"That's right."

"Well, things have changed since then. Gotten worse," she said.

"How have they gotten worse?"

"When I last saw you, things were hard, but since two dogs that were boarding with me were stolen within two days, people are wary about me and the clinic."

"I can't believe that," he said gently.

"Unfortunately, it's true. Since the first one went missing from the barn, exactly one person has kept an appointment with me. Everyone else has canceled. People aren't sure what to think about all of this. And honestly, I can't really blame them. Can you?"

"It's not as if you stole the dogs," he protested.

"That doesn't matter. They were entrusted to my care and the care of my practice, and now they're missing. That puts me at fault. And their owners need someone to blame, since we don't know who took them."

"I'm so sorry. That's not fair to you at all."

Unable to trust her voice not to crack, Harriet remained silent.

He hesitated for a moment and then sat up straight, clearly preparing to rise. "I'll speak to some members of the congregation before next Sunday's service. Encourage them to continue bringing their pets to your clinic."

She caught his sleeve. "I don't want people to come because you shame them into it. I don't even want them to come because they feel they owe it to my grandfather, at least beyond the first time. I want them to come because they trust me as a veterinarian."

"You miss him a lot, don't you?"

She blinked back tears. "I do. Now more than ever. My parents in the States too."

"Isn't your Thanksgiving holiday coming up?"

She wiped at her eyes. "It is."

"What's that like?" he asked. "I've seen pictures. I've seen it depicted in movies and on the telly. But what's it really like?"

"It's special," she said. "The touch football game in the backyard, setting the table with the best dishes and other fancy touches, the joking and teasing, hearing what everyone is thankful for that year, and the food—I can't even begin to describe it. It's all wonderful, and the best part is being with those you love."

"It's soon, isn't it?"

"A week from this coming Thursday. But I'm not going home. I had boarders scheduled for that weekend, and I didn't want to turn them down. Not that I think they'll come now." She sank back against the pew. "And I don't want to go anywhere until Nessie, Princess, and Murphy are found."

He set his hand on her shoulder once again. "Then have your family come here to celebrate."

She was shaking her head before he'd even finished his thought. "The tradition is there, at my parents' home. I can't expect everyone to miss out on that because I chose to move so far away."

"Then have your own feast. With Jinny. With your cousins Anthony and Olivia. With their twins."

His idea rattled around in her head for a moment before she dismissed it with a shake of her head.

"Why not?" he asked.

She looked up at him. "I'm not sure you want me to answer that."

"I wouldn't ask if I didn't."

Pushing off the pew, Harriet stood and walked with him to the door. When they reached it, she confessed, "I guess I'm not feeling terribly thankful right now."

As she stepped out of the Land Rover back at the farm, a flash of movement in the vicinity of the barn caught her attention. Instead of giving her pause, she hurried toward it, her hands fisted at her sides. Enough was enough.

"Hello?" she called.

No answer.

She picked up her pace, running full-tilt for the barn. When she reached it, she stopped short, rage flooding through her. She was certain the door had been closed when she left.

And yet it now stood wide open.

"This is private property," she yelled as she scanned the empty kennels, the new roaming pen, and the large food bags securely closed and stored on a wall shelf in the back corner. "Show yourself this instant, or I'll call the police!"

Mike stepped out from behind the kennels, his hands in the air. "Whoa, whoa. It's just me, Doc."

The breath left her in a relieved rush. "Mike, you scared me. I didn't know you were here. I'm so glad it's you and not—well, never mind."

"I can guess what you thought. I'm sorry. I should have realized beforehand." He tugged at the sleeves of his flannel shirt.

She willed her breathing to slow. "It's Sunday, Mike. The Lord's Day. That means you're not supposed to be working."

"I'm not here to work. Not really." He slid his hands into the pockets of his jeans. "I wanted to check on things, you know? The doors, the windows, the grounds. That sort of stuff."

She wanted to protest, to remind him the safety of the grounds was not his concern on his day off, but she couldn't. His presence, simply out of the kindness of his heart, touched her.

"Thank you, Mike," she said. "Your care and concern mean more than I can say. Especially right now, in light of everything that's happened this past week or so."

"Of course. It's my pleasure."

"Would you like to come in for a little while? I was planning to heat up some soup for lunch, and I'd be happy to share."

"Soup sounds nice. Thank you." He motioned to the open door. "I'll get everything closed up and meet you inside in ten minutes or so if that works."

"Wonderful. I look forward to the company." She started toward her house, calling over her shoulder, "Just come on in when you're ready, but be careful not to let Charlie out." Usually, the cat was allowed to roam, but Harriet had been keeping her in the house in light of the animals who'd gone missing in the area. Perhaps she was being paranoid, and Charlie certainly didn't appreciate the confinement, but she wasn't about to risk it.

"I won't," Mike assured her with a grin. "I'm getting pretty good at handling the different animals around here."

Laughing, Harriet unlocked the back door and opened it.

Then she froze as his words sank in.

"No," she whispered, then clamped a hand over her mouth. She ducked inside as her mind replayed a flood of conversations she'd thought nothing of until that moment. Bits and pieces that, on their own, had sounded so innocent and normal yet now seemed anything but.

Mike had knocked on Cindy's door before he'd come to the farm looking for work.

He had denied knowing Nessie until Cindy corrected him in the clinic the morning after she'd been taken. He'd acted as if he didn't know about Nessie's polydactyl trait, but Cindy told everyone she met about it.

Mike had heard an offer made on Nessie's painting while fixing a hole in the gallery roof mere hours before Nessie went missing. He had been the one who'd discovered the broken window in the gallery.

Mike had been there when she'd discovered Princess was missing.

She'd asked him to watch Murphy while she and Polly ran errands. The dog knew him so probably wouldn't have raised the alarm by barking at him later. Say, in the middle of the night or in the very early morning.

She *had* balled up the post-abduction offers on Grandad's painting and left them on the table beside the couch. Mike could have helped himself to them when he'd been in the house for whatever she'd asked him to fix.

"But why?" she wondered aloud.

"My flat isn't much bigger than this pen. And before you hired me, I wasn't sure I could even keep that."

Was that it? Was Mike behind everything? Because he needed money?

Feeling watched, she slanted her gaze toward her grandfather's favorite chair and spotted Charlie blinking back at her sleepily. Maxwell raised his head and moved closer to her.

"I think I've figured it out," she whispered to the pair.

Maxwell stopped at her feet and gazed up at her.

"I'll smother you with attention when this is all over, sweet boy. I promise. But first, we've got a very important lunch to get ready for."

Charlie stood, lowered her front half in a long, protracted stretch, and then jumped off the chair to join Maxwell. "You've got my back, don't you, Charlie? And so will Van when I've gotten enough to call him."

With a heart that was both heavy yet resolute, Harriet made her way into the kitchen. She set a pot on the stove, filled it with Aunt Jinny's hearty chicken noodle soup, and turned on the burner. She set out napkins and spoons, as well as a plate of crackers, and then returned to the stove. When the soup simmered invitingly, she ladled it into two bowls and carried it to the table as the back door opened and Mike stepped inside.

"Soup's ready," she told him.

Mike took off his coat and gloves and laid them across the back of a chair. She studied the gloves for a moment, wondering if they were the same ones he'd worn when he handled the notes, and then made herself nod. She directed him to the empty seat across from her own. "Please. Come sit. My aunt makes the best chicken noodle soup around."

"Thanks, Doc." He settled in the chair. After Harriet said grace, he spooned up a bite of soup, chased it down with a cracker, and appraised her across the table. "I'm guessing there's been no word from the police about anything?"

She pushed a chunk of chicken around her bowl. "No. Nothing."

"Keep the faith, Doc. The person who did this will be caught soon."

"Maybe today even." She winced at the shrillness of her voice.

He eyed her closely before taking another spoonful of soup. "It's clear you didn't grow up here."

Grateful for the change in subject so she could steady her breathing, she nibbled on a cracker. "What gave me away?"

"Well, besides the accent, you don't call me 'mate' every time I see you, for one."

She made herself laugh. "True. But I have to tell you, it's one of my favorite words."

"Then I'll call you 'mate' when *I* see *you*." He ate another spoonful or two of soup. "So, where are you from? What brought you here to England?"

"I grew up in Connecticut with my family, and I came here because I inherited Cobble Hill Farm from my grandfather."

"This farm is quite a place."

She took a sip of water also and hoped he didn't notice her hand shaking. "It's crazy to think you might have been at the farm searching for your hammer around the same time the person who stole Nessie was sliding that note under my door."

His face tightened. "I know. I hate that I didn't catch whoever it was in the act."

An odd sound interrupted their conversation. Charlie batted something across the floor. In a flash, the feline took off in hot pursuit, coming to a crashing stop at the cabinet beneath the sink.

"Charlie?" Harriet asked. "Please tell me that's not a mouse."

Mike laughed. "I wouldn't have thought a vet would be afraid of mice."

"I'm not *afraid* of mice," she said, pushing herself off her chair. "I just don't want them in my kitchen."

She scooted Charlie away from her prey with her left hand and felt around the floor in front of the cabinet with her right. Her hand closed around something round and light and—

"It's a paper ball," she said, opening her palm. With a rush of breath, she realized what she held. Slowly, with her heart hammering inside her chest, she gently unfolded the paper until she was staring down at a man's name, a telephone number, and a very large amount. One of the missing offers for Nessie's painting.

"Doc? Is everything okay?"

She swallowed hard. She was right that she hadn't thrown away the offers. She'd likely left them in ball form on the end table, where Charlie had found that they were mobile—and fun, apparently. Harriet had searched for them, but she'd checked places that she might have left them, not places they might have ended up after being smacked around by a curious cat.

"Can I do something to help? Do you want me to leave? Do you want me to call someone?"

She didn't know what she wanted. She didn't know anything. After all, if she could be so wrong about what had happened to the missing offers, wasn't it possible she was wrong about everything else she thought she'd figured out?

She held up the wrinkled piece of paper with a weak smile. "Sorry. I was just surprised, I think. The mystery of the missing offers has been solved."

"You mean the ones for your grandfather's painting?" he asked.

She nodded. "This is one of them. If it fell prey to Charlie's love of chasing things, I'm quite confident the other one did too."

"You should probably call that constable then, now that you've got proof, right? So he can investigate the person who made that offer?"

Once again, she saw the man her heart told her Mike was—good, kind, hardworking, and reliable. "You're absolutely right. I'll do that when we're done with lunch."

Setting the paper beside her bowl, she sat, ate a spoonful of soup, and relished the way its warmth melted away at the tension in her shoulders.

"Maybe this will be the break we need," Mike said, indicating the wrinkled paper.

"We?"

He ducked his head, red creeping into his cheeks. "Maybe that sounds a bit presumptuous when I've been here such a short time, but I like it here. I like you and Polly, I like your aunt Jinny, and I like the work. I think I'm good at it. I hope I am, anyway."

"It doesn't sound presumptuous at all, Mike. It's how I felt within days of coming here too. And you're very good at the work you do."

Mike leaned back in his seat. "When did you move here, officially?"

"A few months ago, after Grandad died. He left me this home, the gallery, and his clinic."

"And you up and moved your whole life?" he asked.

She fiddled with the handle of her spoon. "The timing was right. I needed a change—both personally and professionally."

He didn't pry, for which she was grateful. While she no longer grieved the broken engagement that had also ended her job in the States, she still didn't exactly enjoy talking about it. "Are you glad you came?"

She sat back, his question heavy on her heart. "If you'd asked me that question two weeks ago, I'd have said yes. But now, I'm not so sure."

"Don't you like the people?" he asked.

"I love the people. I love being close to my aunt, my cousin and his wife, and their twins. I love the many friends I've made since moving here, like Polly and Pastor Will and Doreen Danby and now you."

"I'm happy to be counted among your friends." He took the last bite of his soup. "Do you like your church home?"

"I *love* my church home," she hurried to assure him. "Pastor Will is wonderful. Kind, compassionate, warm—everything you'd want in a pastor."

"Do you enjoy working with the animals at your clinic?"

"I love every moment of that," she said, straightening in her seat. "It's where I feel most alive, and where I feel as if my grandfather is still with me."

"The weather?"

She laughed. "Well, *that* could be better."

He waved a hand. "Fair enough. Are you homesick for your friends and family in the States?"

She sat with his question for a moment. "I miss them, yes. And I know my mom is worried about me being so far away. But we video chat all the time, and sometimes that was all we could do when I lived there too, on account of how busy I was with work and my then fiancé."

"So if you love all those things, why are you second-guessing your decision to come here?" Mike asked.

Harriet gathered their empty bowls and carried them to the sink, her steps heavy. "Because I can't help but feel as if I've cast a shadow over everything my grandfather worked so hard to achieve."

"How have you done that?"

"His once-thriving veterinary practice hasn't exactly been thriving the last few days."

"That's not your fault. Bad things are happening around here. You're not causing them."

"Other people don't seem to see it that way."

Mike rotated his chair so he faced the sink and Harriet. "So do something else."

"I don't want to do something else." She put the bowls in the sink and filled them with water to soak. "I want to run this clinic. For my grandfather, and for me."

"Say that again."

She grabbed a dish towel from beneath the sink and dried her hands. "Say what again?"

"What you want to do."

"I want to run this clinic."

"For who?"

She leaned against the counter at her back, the reason for his questions suddenly clear. "For my grandfather, and for me."

"Then don't stop, Doc. Find a way to make it good again." Rising to his feet, Mike swept his hand toward the cleared table. "I should be on my way, but thank you for this—the invite, the good food, and especially the conversation. It's nice to sit at a table and connect. That's not something I get to do all that often."

As she walked him to the door and waved goodbye, Harriet reflected on how just a few minutes could completely change a mind.

CHAPTER TWENTY-TWO

Harriet wasn't entirely sure how long she'd sat there with Charlie on her lap and Maxwell snuggled in beside her without his cart, gazing through the French doors at a garden she wasn't really seeing. All she knew with certainty was that daylight had given way to dusk as snippets from past Thanksgivings filtered through her thoughts.

The laughter.

The food.

The closeness.

"It's nice to sit at a table and connect. That's not something I get to do all that often."

She closed her eyes as Mike's words continued to resonate.

"Then have your family come here to celebrate."

Was Will right? Could she have Mom and Dad come? Was it too late to ask?

Harriet leaned across the sleeping feline and picked up her phone. "There's only one way to find out, right, guys?"

Maxwell lifted his head and upper body but relaxed again at Harriet's touch. "Keep resting, sweet boy. Calls with Mom can go long."

She held the phone above Charlie's curled body, mentally calculated her time zone in relation to Connecticut's, and scrolled down to her parents' image on her contact list.

Her mom answered right away. "Harriet!"

Her mom's enthusiasm, coupled with the comfort of her familiar voice, brought an instant smile to Harriet's lips. "Hi, Mom. I didn't catch you at a bad time, did I?"

"There's never a bad time for you to call, sweetheart. Ever."

Closing her eyes, she breathed in her mother's love from an ocean away. "Thanks, Mom. You just got out of church, right?"

"We did."

"Heading to the diner for brunch?" she asked.

"We are."

She swallowed hard. "I miss their blueberry pancakes."

"You could have them if you came back. There's a cute house for sale about ten miles from us. Right, Arthur?"

A low rumble in the background let her know her father was near, even if she couldn't make out his answer.

"Hi, Dad," she called.

"Hi, sweetie," he called back. "It's a good place in nice shape. Not cramped, but not too big. Fairly priced."

Harriet forced another smile and hoped it surfaced in her voice. "I have a house. You know that."

"You can't fault us for missing you, Harriet," her mom said. "Not that we want you to fail or anything. I know how important Grandad's work is to you, and we're so proud of you. We just want to make sure you always know you can come home if it's not the right fit."

Charlie stretched, stood, slowly turned, and then flopped down on her opposite side. "Bought your turkey yet?" Harriet asked.

"We did."

She closed her eyes. "Vegetables picked out?"

"Carrots and corn on the cob, as usual."

"What? No creamed spinach?" she joked.

"You're the only one who ever ate it, Harriet." There was no guilt trip in her mom's voice because that wasn't her way, but Harriet still felt a twinge.

Resting her head against the back of the couch, she made herself ask, "You're still making a peanut butter chocolate pie, right? Because everyone likes that."

"I am. Though your father and I wish you could be here to eat it too."

So do I, she wanted to blurt out. But she refrained. Telling her parents everything that was going on and how badly she needed a hug would cause them to worry. She was an adult. She'd made the choice to leave and take up residency on the other side of the Atlantic Ocean. She would deal with the consequences of that choice herself.

"Harriet? Are you still there?"

Shaking herself back into the moment, Harriet murmured, "I'm here."

"Is everything okay, sweetheart? I feel like I'm picking up something in your voice. Is it homesickness, or is something else going on?"

Nessie, that cat Grandad loved so much, was stolen. Someone broke into Grandad's gallery and took the painting he made of her. Not one, but two boarders were stolen on my watch. And I can't get clients to keep their appointments because of everything that's happening.

I'm failing, both myself and Grandad. The thought nearly tore a sob from her throat.

Instead of saying any of that, she redirected the conversation where she needed it to go—away from her current reality. "You're not going to put anything weird in the stuffing, right?"

She heard her mother relay her question and then her father's answering protest in the background.

"He says—"

"Mushrooms are not weird," she finished for her mother. "I know. He says it every year."

"Which is exactly why I always make two kinds of stuffing—one with mushrooms, one without."

"And I thanked God every year that you did," Harriet joked, even as she felt her eyes beginning to fill. "Anyway, I would imagine you're pulling into the parking lot at the diner right about now, so I'll let you go."

"Wait. Did you get my card?"

"What card?" Harriet asked.

"I sent you a just-because card, with a little something special inside it." A low rumble in the background of the call made Harriet's mother correct herself. "*We* sent you a card. With a little something extra."

Harriet glanced toward the kitchen and the front door beyond, her mind sifting through the events of the past week. Not once, during everything that was happening, had she checked the mailbox.

"It was supposed to arrive yesterday. I hope it didn't get lost."

Wedging the phone between her shoulder and her cheek, Harriet slid her hands under Charlie and gently transferred the sleeping cat to the empty cushion beside Maxwell. "Things have been a little crazy around here, and I don't think I've checked the mailbox in a few days."

"You *are* making sure to eat, right?"

She stood. "I am. I just haven't checked the mail. I'll do that now."

"Good. I love you, Harriet."

Another low rumble in the background made her laugh. "I love you, Dad!" she called, smiling when she could make out his reply. "And I love you too, Mom. Thanks in advance for the card. I'm sure I'll love it."

She ended the call and headed out into the perfectly still evening. With the limited light streaming onto the sidewalk from the windows behind her, Harriet followed it to the mailbox and popped open its door.

"Oh boy," she said at the stack of envelopes and flyers that served as proof of her scatteredness the past few days. She reached into the box, pulled out the contents, and began thumbing her way through the stack.

One by one she flipped past bills and ads until, second from the bottom, she spotted a yellow greeting card envelope bearing her mom's penmanship, which she would have known anywhere.

She worked her finger beneath the seal and tugged out a card with the drawing of a bright yellow sun above the words *Missing You Always.*

"I miss you guys too," she whispered as she opened the card and read the accompanying note.

> *We hope this card makes you smile today, Harriet.*
> *Use this money to get yourself a hot cocoa or some other treat. You deserve it.*
> *Love,*
> *Mom and Dad*

She read the words again, smiled, and tucked the money back inside. Then she examined the last item in the stack, a plain white envelope bearing only her name. Curious, she turned it over, slid her finger beneath the seal, and—

Her phone vibrated inside her pocket. Harriet returned the envelope to the stack and took out her phone with her free hand. She read the name on the screen and quickly accepted the call. "Hey, Polly."

"Hey, boss. I wanted to check in and see how you're doing."

"I'm okay." She made her way back up the sidewalk toward the house. "Did Van tell you I stopped by the station to see him after lunch today?"

"He didn't. Did something else happen?"

"No." She stepped inside, closed the door, and carried the mail into the kitchen. "Well, nothing bad, anyway. I found the offers."

"You did? Where?"

"Apparently, Charlie got hold of them at some point and has been batting them around the house. I caught her with one while I was having lunch with Mike. I found the other one pretty quickly once I knew to search for it from Charlie's perspective."

"I knew you'd find them."

"I'd actually started to believe I wouldn't. But I'm glad I was wrong. Very, very glad."

"Me too," Polly agreed. "Now Van can contact the people who made the offers and figure out whether they're involved."

"Exactly right."

Harriet pulled out a chair and sat down with the stack of mail, her attention falling on the envelope she'd placed on top. There, with the benefit of the overhead light, she looked at her name written in block letters across the front and felt her mouth go dry. "Oh no," she whispered.

"Harriet?"

She heard her name, even registered the worry behind it, but in that moment, all she could think about, all she could do, was rip open the envelope and pull out the single folded piece of paper she knew would be inside.

> *I know you're used to everything going your way,*
> *but for once it's going mine.*
> *You want Nessie?*
> *You want your grandfather's painting?*
> *You want those two dogs?*
> *Then you'll have to pay.*
> *Place fifty thousand pounds in this envelope and*
> *leave it where the polydactyl was found.*
> *Call the police, and you can say goodbye to all of them.*

She heard herself gasp. Heard the jingle of Charlie's bell as the feline jumped off the couch.

As the room began to spin, Harriet grabbed hold of the table's edge and worked to steady her breathing, without much success.

"Harriet?" Polly's voice rose.

She reread the words written in the same large block letters as her name and the previous notes.

"Harriet?" Polly cried. "Say something, please!"

She drew in a shuddering breath. "Where is Van now? Do you know?"

"I'm pretty sure he's at his house. Why?"

"I need him to come here. Now!" She stared at the last line in the letter, her throat constricting. "But please, Polly, he can't say anything to anyone, or we might never see Nessie, Princess, or Murphy again."

CHAPTER TWENTY-THREE

H ow could I have been so careless as to not check my mail for three whole days?" Harriet stepped around Maxwell on the way to the back door and stared out toward the road.

Polly sighed from her spot on the couch. "Maybe you were a bit preoccupied."

"Have *you* forgotten to check the clinic's mailbox the past three days?"

"No, but my home and business haven't been under attack for over a week. Besides, the note said the *two* dogs, right?" Polly asked.

Harriet paced back to the fireplace. "Yes."

"Then that letter couldn't have been in your mailbox any sooner than yesterday."

"Why do you say that?"

"Because Murphy went missing yesterday morning."

She stared at her friend. "You're right. I can't believe I didn't think of that."

"Like I said, you've had a lot going on."

Harriet resumed pacing. "Why does this person think I have access to fifty thousand pounds?"

"I have no idea. But don't worry. Van is going to figure this out."

"The note said no police, Polly. I've taken quite a chance telling Van about this."

"The note writer didn't leave you much choice, giving you evidence in an active criminal case. If you didn't give it to the police, it could be obstruction of justice."

Polly patted the empty spot next to her on the couch. "Come sit before you wear a hole in the floor."

Groaning, Harriet wandered over, stared at the spot Polly indicated, and grudgingly plopped down on it. "I think anyone in my shoes would be crazy at this point."

"Possibly," Polly conceded. "But Van and the rest of his department are working around the clock on this, and they'll get to the bottom of it even if we can't."

Harriet heard the sarcastic lilt in her answering laugh but was powerless to stop it. "Or Candace will somehow get her hands on this latest development, and *everyone* will know. And if that happens, we'll never see Nessie, Princess, Murphy, and Grandad's painting ever again."

"Maybe, maybe not."

She slanted a questioning eye at Polly. "What does that mean?"

"You heard Candace yesterday afternoon. I think she really wants things to work out for you. So maybe if we tell her about the note, she can help us figure something out."

"That doesn't mean she wouldn't use it to her advantage. She has a grandfather to impress too, remember?"

"She does," Polly said. "And that's why I think she'll be happy to help. A surprise wrap-up to the case could make her career."

Harriet realized what Polly was actually suggesting. "Wait, you're right. If she helps us, we could allow her and Doug to be hiding somewhere when everything goes down, giving her the snappy ending she needs to get her promotion."

Polly nodded. "Exactly."

Harriet considered it. "But do you think Van would be upset if we tell Candace about the letter?"

"If her knowing means we have another brain working the problem, I don't see why he would be," Polly said. "She'll just need to get Doug on board about keeping the letter quiet. Which may be hard, since I get the sense he'd like to have Candace moving on sooner rather than later."

The humorous image Polly painted with her words led to a far darker one in Harriet's thoughts. Harriet grabbed her friend's arm. "Could *Doug* be behind all of this?"

Surprise widened Polly's gray eyes.

Before she could reply, Harriet hopped up and paced again. "Not as a way for Candace to get a promotion for herself, but for Doug to rid himself of having to listen to her day in and day out?"

"Are you serious?" Polly asked.

"I think we have to consider every possibility." Now that the idea had pushed its way to the forefront of her thoughts, she had to talk it through. "We thought Candace was amping up the story, but maybe it's been Doug doing it. Maybe this latest note was in my mailbox because he wanted to help Candace's promotion along."

"If you're right, he might not be behind the actual crimes," Polly said. "Not if all he did was write this note to keep things going."

"That's true," Harriet admitted.

"On the other hand, wasn't this note the same as the others?"

She pictured the letter she'd handed to Van little more than an hour earlier. "You mean with the block lettering? Yes. But this one was in an envelope, and the others weren't. Plus, this one was longer. More involved."

"I wonder why an envelope was used this time."

"Van held back details of the notes when Candace asked about them," Harriet mused.

"So if Doug is behind this latest note, he wouldn't have known not to use one." Polly fiddled with a strand of her hair. "Van really is good at his job, isn't he?"

"He is. But I want all of this to be over," Harriet said.

"It will be. Soon."

The conviction in her friend's voice allowed Harriet to relax enough that she was able to return to the couch. "I'm thinking about all of this nearly every minute of every day. And if I manage to push it away for a little while by doing something else, it always finds its way back into the forefront of my thoughts. Just this morning I thought I heard Murphy barking, and it sounded like he was close by."

Polly's mouth gaped. "Where? When?"

"This morning, before church." Wedging herself into the couch corner opposite Polly, Harriet wiggled her fingers to invite Charlie onto her lap. "It turned out I was projecting what I wanted to hear onto what I was actually hearing."

"What were you hearing?"

"Wilson, Theresa Wallace's parrot."

"If you'd told me she was coming in for an emergency visit, I'd have come in to help," Polly scolded.

Harriet waved away her friend's concern. "I offered to stop by her place before church so I could observe Wilson in his own surroundings at the time of day when his behaviors are most prevalent."

"How was he?"

"Let's just say I can see why Theresa is desperate for answers. The sounds he makes would grow quite tiresome, especially with how frequently he makes them and how often he repeats them. But his symptoms have convinced me more than ever that he's stressed about something." Harriet scratched Charlie under the chin, and the cat purred loudly. "He even plucked another feather out right in front of us."

"It's been a couple of weeks since they got here, right? Shouldn't he be adjusted to the move by now?"

"It certainly seems that way, yes. But maybe he was picking up on Theresa's stress when she was struggling to come up with a plot for her next book. Or the stress she clearly has over the dump she's renting."

Polly shot up off the couch with a squeal that brought an end to Charlie's purring. "Are you saying what I think you're saying?"

Charlie jumped to the floor and stalked away.

Harriet chuckled. "I don't know. What do you think I'm saying?"

"That Theresa has officially started writing the next book?"

"Ah, yes, she has."

"When did she start?" Polly pressed her hands to her smiling cheeks. "How far has she gotten?"

"Sometime this past week, I think. And she said the words are really starting to flow. Beyond that, I've got nothing."

Polly bounced on her toes with excitement. "I heard her on a podcast once. Her writing process is fascinating. Where she gets her ideas, how she acts out certain mannerisms and details so she can create them on the page as authentically as possible, the way she keeps herself motivated, the mountain of candy corn she consumes when she's racing toward her deadline, the research she does to get her settings to feel so real—all of it. I actually sent her a bag of candy corn when she was finishing up last year's book."

Harriet laughed. "Seriously?"

Polly grinned. "Oh yes. I wanted her to have what she needed to finish. You really should try her books."

"I will, but you know I prefer mysteries," Harriet said. She sat up straight. "And one thing all mysteries have in common is that they start with a motive. Like you thought Tarquin had in Nessie's disappearance."

Polly licked her lips. "So does that mean Tarquin is back on the list?"

"No, because the painting behind Emerson's door wasn't the one Grandad did." Harriet watched Charlie sniff her way around the pile of firewood while Maxwell wrestled with a toy inside the entryway to the kitchen. "Honestly? Dale Renner fit way better as a suspect than Tarquin ever did, because of his anger with me. But, as we both know, he wasn't our man either."

Polly fell silent.

"What are you thinking?" Harriet prodded.

"I'm thinking that if everything *is* related, you're not the only common denominator."

Startled, she studied her friend, waiting. "I'm listening."

"You grandad is another one."

"How could he be?"

203

Polly met Harriet's gaze. "He's the one who rescued Nessie. He's the one who painted the missing picture. He cared for Princess long before you did. And Murphy's owner brought their previous dog to him."

Silence fell between them as Harriet dissected Polly's words.

"You know what?" Polly flapped a hand. "Ignore what I just said. It's crazy. Doc Bailey may have a connection to all of this, but no one would target him. He was loved by everyone."

"Everyone except Felix Burton," Harriet murmured.

"Who is dead as well." Polly yawned.

Harriet glanced at the mantel clock and cringed. "Oh, Polly, I'm so sorry. I've taken up every last bit of your Sunday evening."

Polly yawned again. "I came because I wanted to, and I stayed because I care. There's nowhere else I'd rather have spent my evening."

Harriet squeezed her friend's hand. "I thank God every day for the blessing of your friendship. But you need your own life, which is why I'm going to pose the notion of taking the day off tomorrow. We don't have any patients, after all."

"Absolutely not. I will be here as scheduled."

"Polly, I—"

Her assistant folded her arms across her chest and glared at Harriet. "No, we need to keep up appearances. People trust a busy vet, or at least one who's ready for anything. If someone has a pet emergency tomorrow, we'll be here to handle it, and that will help turn the tables in our favor. Case closed."

Sighing, Harriet stood. "Oh, how I wish that were true."

CHAPTER TWENTY-FOUR

Harriet had just flipped on the lights inside the clinic Monday morning when a flash of movement outside the front door rooted her feet to the floor. A glance at her watch confirmed what she already knew—Polly wasn't due to arrive for another thirty minutes, and it was far too early for anyone to be slinking around Cobble Hill Farm. Besides, Polly had a key, and a client with an emergency probably would have called.

She made sure her phone was in her pocket, even as anger rose up inside her. Cobble Hill Farm was her home. It was Aunt Jinny's home. And she refused to live in fear.

Her mind made up, she pulled out the phone, held her finger over the entry for the local police, and flung open the door. "I don't know who you are or why you're here, but this is private property and—*Candace?*"

Candace motioned from her thick-rimmed eyeglasses and messy ponytail to her jeans and oversize sweatshirt. "Sorry, it's me. Or, rather, me when I'm not on camera. I didn't mean to startle you."

Harriet scanned the parking area behind the reporter for a news van but didn't see it. "Where is Doug? And why are you sneaking around?"

"Doug isn't here. I'm on my own time. And I'm waiting to talk to you, not sneaking."

"Oh? What can I do for you?" Harriet stepped out into the chilly morning air.

Candace pushed her glasses up the bridge of her nose and quickly closed the gap between them. "Polly reached out to me last night and filled me in about the ransom note you found in your mailbox."

Harriet clenched her jaw, resolving to have a stern talk with her friend. "Polly had no business doing that."

"I'm glad she did. I want to help."

Harriet raised a dubious eyebrow at her. "*Off* camera?"

"For now, yes. But when it all wraps up, I want an exclusive on everything and anything I can get related to what we both hope is a happy outcome."

"And Doug is on board with this?"

"I'm not telling Doug."

"You think he'd push you to break the story that there was another note and that this one is actually demanding money?"

Candace's eyes widened. "They asked for money? How much?"

Harriet grimaced. "Polly didn't tell you that?"

"No, she didn't."

"Does that mean you no longer want to help off camera?"

Candace said nothing for a moment, her makeup-free eyes giving no indication of her thoughts.

"Please," Harriet said. "I'm begging you to keep this under wraps. It could make the difference between seeing and never seeing Nessie, Princess, and Murphy again."

"Not to mention your grandfather's painting," Candace added.

"My grandfather would be the first one to say the animals are way more important." Harriet wandered over to the bench where Doug had filmed her conversation with Aunt Jinny. "And he'd be right."

"Do you remember what the note said?" Candace asked as she lowered herself onto the bench beside Harriet.

"Do you truly want things to work out for me?"

"I do."

"Then yes, I remember what it said. It's burned into my memory."

Candace tugged her tote bag off her shoulder, fished around inside, and pulled out a notebook and a pen. "You say it, I'll write it, and then we'll rip it to shreds—metaphorically speaking, that is."

Harriet stared out at the parking lot, as she slowly, painstakingly, dictated the words from the note. "'I know you're used to everything going your way, but for once it's going mine. You want Nessie? You want your grandfather's painting? You want those two dogs?'"

"'Those two dogs?'" Candace echoed. "That's how it was worded?"

"Yes. And then it went on. 'Then you'll have to pay. Place fifty thousand pounds—'"

Candace gave a long, low whistle. "That's a lot of money."

"I know."

"I'm sorry." Candace paused the pen above her notepad, ready to write once again. "Keep going, if you can."

"'Place fifty thousand pounds in this envelope and leave it where the polydactyl was found.'" She stopped and swallowed hard.

"Is that it?"

"No. I just needed a moment before I could tell you the last line. 'Call the police, and you can say goodbye to all of them.'"

Candace finished writing and held the notebook out to Harriet. "Read it through and see if I got everything you said."

Harriet took the spiral-bound book and skimmed the ugly words. "Yes, this is right."

"Is it close enough, or do you think it's exact?"

"It's exact."

Candace leaned close, her lips moving as she reread the words. "Okay, two things stand out to me right off the bat. First, whoever wrote this note used Nessie's name, but not Princess's or Murphy's. Next, he or she tells you to put the money where Nessie was found, which makes me think the writer was involved with Nessie's rescue six years ago. Plus, they knew she was a polydactyl."

"I think the only real clue is the first thing you mentioned," Harriet said, tapping the sentence with her finger. "My grandfather's painting not only showed Nessie before she was rescued, it also showed the place where she was found. And that painting was prominently hung in a public gallery for six years. And everyone knew she was a polydactyl, because not only did her owner tell everyone that tidbit, but you yourself have shared it with your viewers multiple times in the past week."

"I guess you're right about all that," Candace said, crestfallen.

"And the local paper did a whole write-up on the rescue, with a photograph of the place Nessie was found. That article and picture are both available online to anyone who searches for either my grandfather or Nessie."

Candace scooted back on the bench. "That's true," she said. "I'd forgotten that. I know the article and the picture well, thanks to such a search."

Harriet tapped her chin with a finger. "But what you pointed out about the two dogs part raises some questions, at the very least."

"What questions?" Candace asked.

"It makes me wonder if the person who has them doesn't know their names." Harriet twisted on the bench so she could gauge Candace's reaction at what she said next. "Like Doug, for instance."

"You mean *my* Doug?"

"I do. He made it clear in a recent conversation with Polly and me that he didn't know the missing dogs' names—well, at least Princess's."

Candace scowled. "I knew their names, so Doug should've known them too." She thought for a moment. "I told him a couple of days ago that reporting the discovery of another note—especially a true ransom note—would be the shoo-in I needed to make the powers that be offer me the weekend anchor job."

"And then a true ransom note was found in my mailbox. Written in the same block lettering he probably already knew about from when you talked to the police. But this time it was in an envelope."

"Does that mean the other two *weren't* in envelopes?"

"That's correct. Just this latest one."

"Which it would need to be in order to be mailed."

Harriet kept her eyes locked on Candace. "There were no postal markings of any kind."

"So it was put in your mailbox by someone other than a mail carrier."

"I think that's a safe guess."

Candace was quiet for a moment as she seemed to be working her way through everything she'd heard. Finally, she said, "And you think Doug did all of this?"

"I'm thinking he's a good possibility for at least this latest note, if not Princess and Murphy as well."

Candace's expression grew calculating. "Doug had an accident in his personal vehicle en route to an after-hours story a couple weeks ago. While it's in the body shop, the station is allowing him to use the news van when he's not working. Which means if he'd taken either or both of those dogs, there would probably be dog hair in it."

"Do you think you'd have noticed that?"

"I believe I would have. And if I didn't, I'm quite sure *someone* who's ridden in that vehicle would have—one of the anchors, a viewer, a colleague, you name it." Candace folded her arms. "Why would Doug do this anyway? I'm the one who stands to get the promotion, not him."

Harriet waited in silence as Candace's expression moved from confusion to consideration—and then to realization.

"If I get the promotion, he's free of me." Candace unfolded her arms and used her hands to push herself off the bench. "This is crazy. Wait a minute." She snatched up the notebook and studied the note. "Was everything spelled correctly in the actual letter?"

"It was."

"Then I can say with absolute certainty that Doug did not write it."

"You can't know that," Harriet protested.

"Oh yes, I can. Spelling is not Doug's forte. Besides, Doug can hardly pronounce the word *polydactyl*. I'm quite certain he couldn't spell it."

Harriet's gaze dropped back to the line the reporter referenced, and she felt her shoulders sag. "Maybe he looked it up?"

"No. Doug leaves research to the reporters. I'd stake my entire career on the fact that if Doug had written this letter, he'd simply have told you to leave the money where Nessie was found."

She wanted to believe Candace was wrong, that Doug had been a spelling prodigy in his youth, but Candace was sharp. If she said the man couldn't spell, she was probably right.

"Will this nightmare ever end?" With a groan, Harriet planted her elbows on her knees and buried her face in her hands.

Through her fingers, she saw Candace's feet moving as she paced. "Did you know that someone else told your grandfather about Nessie?"

"I assume you're talking about Felix Burton," Harriet said.

"So you knew."

"Yes. Felix spotted Nessie wedged in the rocks and told my grandfather." She straightened then leaned back against the bench. "His part was never acknowledged in any of the articles about the rescue, but that wasn't from lack of trying on my grandfather's part. He always told the reporters and the photographers that Felix was the one who first found Nessie in trouble. But none of them chose to include Felix in the stories they wrote."

Candace shrugged. "I wouldn't have either. The story was in the rescue. People wouldn't have cared about that extra bit of trivia. But this Felix person clearly carried a lot of bitterness about it."

"How do you know?"

"Someone sent me a link to some letters he wrote to the editors of various publications. Letters telling of his part in Nessie's rescue and demanding he be given credit. But very few people read the Letters to the Editor."

"Ouch." Harriet winced in sympathy for Felix's frustration. "Who sent you the link to those articles?"

"I suspect it was the same person who emailed me about one of the huge offers for your grandfather's painting after Nessie's abduction. It was for twenty-two thousand pounds."

Harriet snapped her gaze to the reporter. "That offer was in a sealed envelope."

"Was the amount correct?"

"It was. Who sent you that tip?" Harriet asked.

"I don't know. They didn't give a name."

"But you had their email address, right? Did you try to answer them?"

"I couldn't. The address was totally anonymous and untraceable."

Tires crunched over gravel, and Harriet raised her head to see Polly's car pulling into the parking area. "Good morning, Harriet," Polly sang as she climbed out of the car. Then her gaze fell on the reporter, and her expression dimmed a bit. "Candace."

"Hello, Polly," Harriet replied. "Did you get any other emails, Candace?"

"Several, actually. I got one telling me about the break-in at the gallery, another about Princess, another with links to the bad reviews that were posted about you and the clinic, and another about how Murphy was stolen right out of your home through an unlocked back door."

"Emails?" Polly asked, claiming a spot on the bench next to Harriet. "What emails?"

"Were these emails how you first heard about everything?" Harriet asked Candace.

"Every single time."

"And they were all sent by way of this untraceable address?"

"Actually, they came in under different ones. But yes, they were all anonymous, untraceable, and couldn't receive replies. The accounts might even have been deleted after the emails were sent."

Polly whistled long and low. "That's impressive. Someone must be really dedicated to covering their tracks."

Harriet sat with Candace's answers for a moment, mulling them over in her mind. "I don't understand how someone knew the exact offer I got in a sealed envelope. And who would know about everything that happened early enough to tell you before the official channels?"

Candace looked around. "It seems to me that you have a few people who are here in close quarters with you pretty much every day. We already know that Polly has spoken to me about something without your approval. There's also your aunt, the gallery manager, and the handyman, at least that I know of. Perhaps one of them is emailing me about the goings-on around here. I mean, it might even be your attempt to drum up business for your clinic after those nasty reviews."

Harriet shot up from the bench. "There's no way it's any of them. Why would they? Having you and Doug here almost every day this week has been quite stressful, since we never know when you'll pop up to broadcast what we think are private conversations. They all know that, and they wouldn't feed into it. And I believe in running a business in a way that honors my grandfather. It's definitely not me."

"Excuse me, but I'm right here," Polly interjected. "And I can also assure you that it's not any of us."

"Maybe, maybe not. But you might be surprised at the way some people love to be the ones in the know and therefore the ones to tell everyone else."

Harriet crossed her arms over her chest. "None of the people on this farm are that way."

Candace gave her a mild smile. "Because you've known them all so well for so long, I suppose."

"I've known my aunt my entire life. We've always been close. I've known Polly and Ida the whole time I've lived here. They absolutely wouldn't do something like that."

"No, I would not." Polly stood and rested a bracing hand on Harriet's shoulder. "Nor would Ida."

Candace's blue eyes moved between Harriet and Polly. "And the handyman?"

Harriet waited for Polly to answer with the same conviction as she had for Ida, but Polly remained silent.

Finally, Harriet answered instead. "No. Mike wouldn't tip you off."

"How long has he been working here, Harriet?" Candace asked, switching gears.

Harriet walked to the edge of the sidewalk and stared out at the trees, her thoughts traveling in directions she didn't want to go.

"Harriet?"

"He started right before Nessie went missing," Polly answered for her.

Candace stepped in front of Harriet. "You don't find that timing a little interesting?"

"I did for a little while. But I don't anymore."

Polly frowned at Harriet for a moment then faced the reporter. "Your hair looks good in that ponytail, by the way. You should wear it like that on the telly every now and again."

"I hate to think of the emails I'd get from viewers if I did," Candace said, laughing.

"Why are you here, and dressed so casually?" Polly asked.

"Because you called her about the note in my mailbox," Harriet said, her tone a little sharper than she'd intended.

"We talked about bringing her in on it," Polly said.

"Yes, but I didn't realize we'd made a firm decision."

Candace waved her hands. "Hello? I'm also right here."

Polly laughed. "We know. Annoying, isn't it?"

"For what it's worth, I'm dressed casually because I'm here on my own time to help Harriet figure out what's going on so she can get her happy ending and I can get mine." The reporter turned back to Harriet, her expression earnest. "Which is why I'm asking the tough questions this morning."

Harriet forced a smile. She hadn't appreciated some of Candace's questions, but she couldn't deny that they had been useful. "We'll take all the help we can get."

"Good." Candace frowned at her watch. "I really have to run and get my hair and face ready for my workday. But Harriet, hang in there. I, for one, am rooting for you."

Together, Harriet and Polly watched Candace get into her car, start the engine, and drive away. When she was gone from view, Polly nudged Harriet. "Hearing her confirmation that she's on our side had to feel good, right?"

"It did." Harriet drew in a deep breath, held it for a few seconds, and then slowly released it into the morning air. "But it's well past eight now and time to get inside. To do what, exactly, I'm not sure. But something productive."

Polly followed Harriet into the clinic and greeted both Maxwell and Charlie. When she was done, she pointed beyond her always-neat desk to the waiting area. "I think I'll do a little reorganizing in here to make it even nicer for our customers."

"You mean the customers we don't have?" Harriet stopped and held up her hands. "I take that back. Yes, that sounds like a good idea. Thank you. If you don't mind, I'll leave you to that so I can focus on other things."

"Of course. If you need anything, let me know."

"I will. Thanks." Harriet started toward her office only to stop halfway to the door. "Polly?"

"Yes?" Polly made her way to an end table between chairs and scooped up the magazines on it.

"When Candace suggested that you or Ida or Mike might be behind the anonymous tips she's been getting this week, you stood up for yourself, and you stood up for Ida. But not Mike. Why?"

Polly paused in flipping through the magazines. "I've known Ida longer."

"Fair enough. How many of his references did you call before I hired him?" Harriet asked.

"I didn't call any. You told me you had a good feeling."

Harriet bit her lip. "You think he's good, right? That I made a smart decision hiring him?"

"Of course you did," Polly said, adding two more magazines from another, smaller table to her pile. "He works hard. He's fixed things we didn't even know were problems. And he's always here. My mother has found that quite reassuring this past week."

Harriet drank in the conviction she heard in her friend's voice and used it as the boost she needed to step inside her office and flip on the light switch. "Thanks, Polly."

"My pleasure. But why do you ask? Are you doubting Mike?"

"To be honest, yesterday I had a laundry list of things that made me think Mike was behind everything, including the missing offers."

"The ones you found, thanks to Charlie?"

Harriet leaned against the doorframe. "That's right."

"Why did you think Mike took them to begin with?"

"Because I realized he'd been in the living room the morning after I remembered putting the offers on the table next to the couch."

Polly cocked her head. "And the rest of the things on the list?"

Twenty-four hours earlier, everything she'd come up with had sounded so logical. Yet now, as she prepared to say them aloud for Polly, they seemed silly, even a little contrived. Especially since she no longer suspected any such thing. "Well, Mike had knocked on Cindy's door before he came to the farm."

Polly carried a half-empty jar of peppermint candies to her desk, set it down, and filled it from a bag she kept in the bottom drawer. "Because he was looking for work."

"He denied knowing Nessie until Cindy corrected him in the clinic the morning after she'd been taken," Harriet said.

"'Denied' is a little strong, don't you think?" Polly carried the full jar back to the side table it normally graced and tried it out in various places, turning it to get the perfect angle. "I think he simply didn't remember at first because he'd stopped at so many houses."

"Mike acted as if he didn't know that Nessie was a polydactyl, but Cindy tells everyone she meets about it."

Polly finally found the perfect position for the candy jar and nodded in satisfaction. "Again, he went to a lot of houses and talked to a lot of people. He probably heard a lot of stories."

Harriet went to the candy jar, helped herself to a peppermint, and unwrapped it with a grin at Polly. "Mike was the one who discovered the broken window in the gallery, was there within minutes of me realizing Princess was missing, and knew Murphy would willingly go with him."

"I think he's a diligent guy who needs the work, so he's here early and stays late, hoping you'll keep him around." Polly crossed back to the candy jar and straightened the lid.

Harriet smiled. "I think so too. I wanted to make sure you and I were on the same page about him."

"We certainly are about whether he's behind everything. I don't think that's the case. However, I'm not sure I can say with absolute certainty that he's not the one who tipped Candace off in the immediate aftermath of everything that's happened. Especially since she pointed out that it's likely to be someone who's here all the time. Because I *know* it's not me. And I'm just as positive it's not Ida. So that leaves Mike. Unfortunately."

"I don't want it to be Mike," Harriet protested around the peppermint. "I want to know he's the good guy I believe him to be."

"Me too." Polly crossed back to her desk, slipped on her coat, and hooked her thumb in the direction of the door. "I'm going to head out to the barn and do some tidying out there."

Harriet started to protest, to remind her friend they had no boarders scheduled for the foreseeable future, but she refrained. She had to think positively, for Polly and for herself. So she smiled her agreement and grabbed another peppermint as the door closed in Polly's wake.

She made her way to her office, sat down at her desk, and flipped open her laptop. As the machine whirred to life, she readied her fingers over the keypad and—

"Wait a minute," she said aloud. "Mike can't be the one who sent Candace the tips she told me about. He doesn't know anything about computers. Which means there's no way he's sending email over some specialized anonymous email address, much less several."

She pulled away from her computer as someone's words came back to her.

"Instead, I'm wasting hours researching things like poisonous plants, how to flee to another country, the size of the average US jail cell, anonymous email addresses, and miniature cupcakes."

CHAPTER TWENTY-FIVE

She'd barely left the farm when her phone rang inside the Land Rover's cupholder. Glancing in the rearview mirror at the empty road in her wake, Harriet slowed long enough to hit accept and put the call on speaker.

"Hey, Polly." Harriet drove to the end of the road and took a right. "I didn't have time to come find you in the barn before I left."

"I was hosing out Murphy's kennel when I heard the Land Rover start up," Polly said. "Where are you going?"

"I'm sorry. I thought of something and need to chase it down."

"If you'd given me a heads-up, I could've gone with you," Polly protested.

At the end of the next road, she glanced at the vet manual on the passenger seat and felt her jaw tighten in response. "This is something I have to do alone."

"Okay." Polly sucked in a breath. "Are you planning to ask Mike if he's been tipping off Candace? Because if you are, I'm pretty sure he's working on something behind the gallery. I hear hammering."

"No."

"Should *I* ask him?" Polly asked. "I can do it nicely."

"No."

"Why not?" Polly asked.

Harriet slowed as she passed the church. "Because Mike isn't the one responsible for tipping off Cindy."

"How do you know that?"

She pulled to a stop in front of her chosen destination and cut the engine. "Because I know who is."

"Who?"

"The same person I have a sick feeling is responsible for everything that's happened." Harriet glanced at the tired, run-down cottage and squared her shoulders. "Polly, I have to go."

"Harriet, where are you?"

It was on the tip of her tongue, but she stopped herself. For the time being, anyway. "I can't tell you until I'm sure I'm right."

"Why not?"

"Because I don't want to disappoint you if I don't have to."

"Okay, now you're starting to freak me out. How would knowing your location disappoint me?" Polly asked.

Harriet pocketed her keys and grabbed the book. "If I'm right, you'll understand. In the meantime, keep your phone on you. I'll call you after I call Van."

"*Van?*" Polly echoed. "Harriet, where are you?"

"I'll touch base as soon as I can."

Harriet ended the call and slid out from behind the steering wheel, silenced her phone, and stuck it in her back pocket. She tucked the book under her arm, made her way up the sidewalk, and knocked on the scarred, brown door.

She waited a minute before she knocked again.

As she was contemplating her next move, the door finally opened, and Theresa Wallace peeked out.

"Oh, Harriet. I must have lost track of time." Theresa pulled the door open to reveal more of her pajama-clad body and ruffled hair. "Actually, did I know you were coming?"

"You didn't, and I'm sorry to drop by unannounced, but I'm chasing down a hunch." Harriet showed Theresa the bird manual, reflecting that she wasn't technically lying. She was simply pursuing something else, though she wouldn't be upset if there was a breakthrough about Wilson too.

Any resistance she thought she saw in the author's eyes quickly gave way to a genuine smile. "Well, I'd be a fool to pass up a house call," Theresa said, opening the door wide enough for Harriet to pass through.

"How is he this morning?" she made herself ask as Theresa closed the door behind them. "Any new sounds?"

Theresa lifted a small white box into the air and gave it a little shake. "I haven't heard anything on his monitor yet."

"That's a good sign, right?"

Theresa's tired laugh became a long, loud yawn. "We'll see. He hasn't seen me yet today, so that might be why I haven't heard anything."

"Did I wake you?" At Theresa's sheepish nod, Harriet pointed at the door. "I'm sorry. I can come back in a little while if you'd prefer."

"No. Now is fine. I would've been awake an hour ago if I hadn't gotten on a writing roll that lasted until three o'clock in the morning." Theresa yawned again. "But it's okay. It's time to get up and on with my day."

"You're sure?" Harriet asked.

"I am. But would it be terribly ungrateful of me if I asked to meet you at Wilson's cage in a few minutes?" Theresa gestured at her pajamas. "I need to put myself together a little."

"Of course not." Harriet pointed down the hall. "Is he where he was when I saw him yesterday?"

"He is." Theresa held out the little white box. "Can you take the monitor with you so I don't forget it somewhere? I'm half awake at best."

"Of course."

Slowly, Harriet made her way into the room she'd visited the previous day, her gaze falling on the bird perched on a bar in the center of the cage. "Well, hello there, Wilson. How are you doing this morning, sweet boy?"

Wilson untucked his head from his wing and launched into the series of sounds he'd made the previous morning.

She set the handset on Theresa's desk and crossed to the cage. "I remember those sounds. I'm not sure what you're trying to tell us with them, but you've got my attention." She pulled out her phone. "I'm going to record you, so give it your best."

Wilson went through the sounds again.

"You'll be okay, Wilson," she said, lowering her voice and putting her phone away. "No matter what happens, I'll make sure you're okay. I promise you that."

Once more, Wilson ran through his sounds, rocking from side to side as he did. When he reached the end, he began again.

"I was wondering how on earth I managed to sleep so late with him carrying on like this, and now I know."

Harriet jumped at the sound of a voice behind her. Theresa had joined her sooner than she'd expected.

Her hostess was indicating a white box on the screened-in porch. It was larger than the one Harriet had brought into the room. "Last night after dinner it got too chilly to sit out there any longer, so I moved everything in here—my notes, my computer, and Wilson," Theresa continued. "Clearly, I forgot the transmitter for his monitor. Sorry, buddy. Have you felt ignored all morning?"

Harriet glanced back at the cage to find Wilson studying her. "Mistakes happen," she murmured.

Wilson's symphony began again.

Theresa ran her hands over her face with a groan. "I can't tell you how many times I've tried to play out a scene for this book in my head. Every time I almost have it down, Wilson starts in with his sounds again. And then, suddenly, instead of the romantic café or soul-cleansing beach walk I was trying to visualize for my main character, all I can see is this old, dilapidated space."

Her gaze still fixed on Wilson, Harriet willed her voice to remain casual. "I was thinking about your research in preparation for a new book."

"That's one of my absolute favorite parts. Though trying out the stuff I research can be quite fun too, like living in London the past six months. Even though I didn't know what my plot was going to be until this week, I knew I wanted it set in England. Immersing myself in life here will help make my book more authentic."

Harriet watched as Wilson turned his back, rocked for a few seconds, and then stared down at the bottom of the cage. "Those searches you mentioned earlier, like poisonous plants and fleeing the country. Do you actually try that stuff out?"

Theresa laughed. "Well, obviously, not those particular ones. Usually I don't have time to go off on rabbit trails. Especially when I'm on deadline. My focus needs to be on the book I *have* to write, not the one I *want* to write."

When it was clear Wilson wasn't going to speak again, Harriet faced Theresa. "They can't be one and the same?"

The author wrinkled her nose. "Not according to my agent and my publisher."

"I don't understand."

"I'm known for romance novels. The happily-ever-after tales that land me on bestseller lists for weeks at a time both here and in the United States."

"And you can't be known for writing a thriller?" Harriet asked.

Theresa laughed again, earning her a fleeting glance from Wilson. "I could be if they'd let me. But I've been told in no uncertain terms to stay in my lane."

"That must be frustrating."

"It is if I allow myself to dwell on it for too long. But I make good money writing what they want. And, as a result, I can opt to work in places like this." Scrunching her nose, Theresa shook her head. "Not this specific building, you understand, but in villages like White Church Bay in all sorts of different countries."

"True. And if my friend, Polly, is any indication of how your readers feel about you and your books, you're adored."

Theresa leaned back against the edge of her paper-strewn desk. "I'm grateful for her and everyone like her. Truly."

"But you really want to write the thriller," Harriet guessed.

"I do." Theresa rolled her shoulders a few times then gave a hearty sigh. "I humor myself by doing a little research for it every now and again in the hope I'll hit on a plot so sensational my agent will *beg* me to write it. But so far, I've had no luck."

Harriet pointed at the darkened computer screen. "What about sending anonymous emails? Did you research that?"

Theresa made a face. "The whole email stuff was too hard for me to figure out on my own." She glanced at her watch. "I know all sorts of people in all kinds of fields. I can call one or more of them to help me make sense of things. But I can't even think about doing that until I've written and delivered my current work in progress."

Harriet tried to hide her disappointment. There went her possible lead. If Theresa hadn't been able to figure out the emails, there was no way she was Candace's anonymous source. "Did you end up going with an animal theme for the book you're writing?"

Theresa pushed away from her desk and wandered over to Wilson's cage. "I didn't. I was thinking I'd go with a couple where one of them likes animals and the other doesn't. But I have to like both my hero and heroine. I have to want them to be together by the end, and so do my readers. I wasn't liking him at all, which means my readers wouldn't have either."

"Why not?" Harriet prodded.

"Because right from the jump, he had issues with people who had pets. And even though I knew that would change at some point because of the heroine, I didn't like him. You can give your hero and heroine a redemption arc so that your readers will root for them by the end, but he was so unpleasant that I couldn't come up with a steep enough arc to redeem him." Theresa studied her bird silently for a moment. "Some of that may have been because I was seeing whoever stole those dogs from your clinic in him. But even if I wasn't, I don't want to spend the first third of a book with a character who dislikes animals. It puts me in too negative a space."

Harriet may have nodded, maybe even offered an understanding word or two, but all she was aware of was the disappointment coursing through her body. Not that she had particularly relished the idea of disappointing Polly or having the stressed Wilson witness his owner being led off in handcuffs. But she was ready for things to return to normal—for Nessie, Princess, and Murphy to be reunited with their owners, for her grandfather's painting to be returned to the gallery, and for the clinic to continue growing under her guidance and care.

"Do you think I should break my lease and move back to Massachusetts so Wilson can get better? Because I will in a heartbeat if you think it would help him."

Harriet met Theresa's worried eyes across the top of Wilson's cage and silently chastised herself for the suspicion that had brought her there. "I don't think so. Not yet, anyway. Let's give him a few more days and see—"

She stopped, startled, and scanned the room.

"What is it?" Theresa asked.

"I thought I heard Pastor Will's voice."

"I didn't hear anything."

Harriet held her finger to her lips. "There it is again. Listen."

Will's familiar and comforting tone reached her ears. "This Sunday we're having a pancake breakfast after service, Theo. It would be a great place for you to connect with people who may have known your mum or even your granddad."

Theresa came out from behind the cage to stand beside Harriet. "I heard him that time."

"Good. I was beginning to question my sanity," Harriet joked.

"I hope you'll give it some thought, Theo."

Theresa grabbed the handset from her desk. "We're hearing him on *this*."

"How?" Harriet asked.

Theresa pointed to the system's transmitter on the screened-in porch. "Because of *that*."

Harriet took in the series of small lights that flickered as Will spoke again. Then she peered beyond the transmitter to the handsome minister strolling along a narrow alleyway at the edge of Theresa's yard. "That's an impressive gadget."

"I spent a lot for it, so I would hope so."

"If you don't need anything else from me, I'd like to go say hello," Harriet said to her. "I'll leave you to your day, okay?"

"That's fine." Theresa opened the door to the porch for Harriet. "Thanks for stopping by to check on Wilson. It means more than you know."

Feeling heat in her cheeks at the real reason for her visit, Harriet hurried out into the morning air.

The porch door closed behind her with a smack, drawing Will's attention. He turned toward her with a smile that set butterflies fluttering in her stomach. "Harriet?"

"Hi, Will."

He picked his way around clumps of dead grasses and misshapen bushes to grasp her hand. "This is a nice surprise. What brings you to this neck of the woods?"

"I stopped by to see Theresa Wallace and her parrot, Wilson."

He took in the cottage behind her then tilted his head in the direction he'd come from. "I did the same for one of our other parishioners."

She squinted at the slightly larger but still gray and run-down home. "I think I recognize that place. But it can't be the one I'm thinking of, because that one is on Rocky Shore Drive."

Will pointed to the snippet of road just visible at the edge of Theresa's property. "This road connects with Rocky Shore Drive between these two houses."

"I see." That must mean the dilapidated shed she'd seen from Theresa's window the previous day, which she now saw had three locks lining the door, belonged to Theo. "I didn't know Theo went to our church."

"You've met him?" Will asked.

"Briefly. Polly played a round of darts with him at the Crow's Nest a few days ago. I met him when I gave him a ride home because it was raining."

Will's gaze traveled back to the man's home. "I wonder if that's why he's been smiling the past few days. Because he's getting out and about and finally making connections with people."

"Maybe." She shrugged. "And maybe now that Dale Renner is no longer angry with me about Scout, Theo will decide I'm worth trying to make a more positive connection with as well."

"I'm glad you've resolved things with Dale. I know that was weighing on you. Are he and Theo friends?" Will asked.

"I'm not sure I'd go that far. Dale's usual darts partner didn't show the other night, so Theo volunteered to play with him. The evening newscast came on while they were there. Since that was the last segment before Princess and Murphy went missing, people still felt empathy for me. Candace Moore's cameraman helped me gain even more with a candid moment he captured between Aunt Jinny and me."

Will flinched. "Which angered Dale even further, I'm guessing?"

"It did. And Polly seems to think Theo was swept up in it that night because he was partnered with Dale."

"And then you met Theo yourself?"

"Polly and I were driving through town during a particularly heavy downpour when she pointed him out on the sidewalk. He was walking without an umbrella. So I offered him a ride. He knew who I was from the story he'd seen on TV at the Crow's Nest, and he was rather challenging about my home, my grandfather, and me personally. Polly tried to explain it away as Dale's influence, but it was still unsettling."

The sparkle faded from Will's eyes, replaced by concern. "I'm sorry he treated you that way, Harriet. I'm saddened to hear about it but not surprised. Just be yourself, and hopefully he'll come around."

Something about Will's tone and his words about not being surprised hit her. "Am I forgetting something where this man is concerned? Did I meet him earlier and I'm not remembering? Did I say—or fail to say—something that hurt him?"

"No, Harriet. Theo Littleton's anger and his bitterness predates you." Will rubbed the back of his neck. "Both of you, actually."

She frowned, somehow even more confused. "Theo Littleton? As in Theresa Wallace's landlord?"

"Yes. Theo inherited the cottage he's renting to Theresa, the cottage he lives in, and the piece of land between them from his grandfather, Felix Burton."

Harriet gasped. "Felix Burton?"

"I take it you've heard about him?"

"I have, courtesy of Aunt Jinny."

"What did she tell you?"

"That Felix Burton despised my grandfather. For being a better student in school, for being popular in White Church Bay, for marrying my grandmother, for being successful in his veterinary career, for all the attention he got for rescuing Nessie, and even for breathing, it seems. And now you're telling me this man's grandson has a problem with me, simply because I'm Harold Bailey's granddaughter?"

Will's answering silence was as clear as any answer he could've given.

"Wow," Harriet said. "I don't know what to say. Or what I'm supposed to do with this."

Will planted his hands on her shoulders and peered into her eyes. "You have enough on your plate right now, Harriet. This thing with Theo is for him to work through, not you. Put it out of your head and know beyond a shadow of a doubt how deeply loved your grandfather was in this town and how deeply loved you are as well."

She nodded, but as she made her way back to the clinic, she had to wonder if it was as simple as he seemed to believe.

CHAPTER TWENTY-SIX

C hocolate caramel shortbread bar?"

Harriet lifted her head from its resting spot on her desk. Polly held a plate of perfectly cut dessert bars, and worry touched every feature in her expression. "Shouldn't you have left hours ago?" she asked.

"Probably." Polly approached Harriet's desk. "You said you weren't hungry for real food when you got back, but I thought maybe you'd feel differently if it was my mum's chocolate caramel shortbread bars."

Harriet inhaled the enticing aroma from the plate. "I could use some prayers, Polly. From your mom too, if she can. Because I'm really struggling right now."

"Done."

"Thank you."

Polly set the plate down beside Harriet. "And in the meantime, you need to eat something to keep up your strength."

Harriet's mind protested even as her stomach rumbled. "How can I, when everything is in ruins?"

"Everything is not in ruins," Polly replied firmly, selecting a bar. "They're going to find Princess and Murphy. And they're going to find Nessie and Doc Bailey's painting too. I just know they are." She broke off a bite and popped it into her mouth.

"Does Van think so?" Harriet asked.

Polly ducked her head then pushed the plate toward Harriet. "Seriously, have one."

"I'll take that as a no," Harriet murmured.

Polly lifted her gaze back to Harriet's. "That doesn't mean he thinks they won't. The two bids you gave him proved to be a dead end. The woman behind the lower bid simply wanted to buy the painting and figured the price would go up. When she heard the painting had been stolen, she was shocked."

Harriet digested the news. "And the man behind the higher bid? I'm guessing there was nothing there either?"

"Van says there's no way of knowing. The phone number written on the offer isn't a working number and hasn't been for more than a year. And the name that was given appears to be a dead end as well."

Harriet perked up. "Which could mean he's our man, couldn't it?"

"It could. But with nothing real to go on, and no prints other than yours and Ida's on the bids, it's not looking good. But remember, the police aren't the only ones trying to figure all this out. We are too."

Harriet took a bar then began to crumble it without putting any of it in her mouth. "For all the good that's doing. I've got nothing. How about you?"

"Me too," Polly admitted. "That doesn't mean Candace won't find something though. Everyone wants this to turn around for you."

Harriet's answering laugh sounded fake, even to her own ears. "Not everyone, as evidenced by the fact that all of this has happened in the first place. And, on top of that, I think there's even someone who's celebrating my trials."

Polly rolled her eyes over the bar she was eating. "Please tell me you're not fussing over this Theo bloke."

"Theo Littleton? I sure am."

Polly snorted. "Someone petty enough to hold a grudge against the granddaughter of a man whose one crime was being a good person doesn't deserve to take up space in your mind."

"I know, but that doesn't change the fact that it stings." Harriet grabbed another shortbread bar from the plate and began to break it apart as well.

Polly laid a hand on hers. "Let it go. You're Harriet Bailey, granddaughter of Doc Bailey. You care about people and their feelings on a different level." She gently took the bar from Harriet's destructive hands. "But it's okay to put this man out of your mind. You can and probably should pray for him if he's celebrating the disappearance of three animals and a family heirloom because of some decades-old grudge that has nothing to do with either of you, but you don't need to let him bring you down."

Before Harriet could reply, the sound of repeated clicking caught her ear. "What's that?"

Polly finished her bar. "Mike's installing dead bolts on the clinic door and your back door. Sounds like he's testing them to make sure everything works properly, like the perfectionist he is. When I offer him a bar, he might actually eat it instead crumbling it to bits."

Harriet sheepishly took a bite of the dessert bar and quickly followed it up with another. "Wow. These are amazing."

"I knew you'd like them."

"You were totally right." She took another bite. "Thank you, Polly. This was very sweet of you."

The clicking sound reached them again.

Polly lifted the plate of treats and motioned them toward the door. "I'm going to take these out to Mike so he can have one before he leaves."

"Tell him I'm pretty sure he's got both the locking and the unlocking down pat," Harriet said with a laugh.

Polly hopped up. "Will do." She disappeared through the office door.

A moment later, Harriet heard Polly offer Mike a chocolate caramel shortbread bar and Mike accept with gratitude.

Suddenly, something clicked into place.

Bolting upright on her chair, Harriet grabbed the manual devoted to birds, quickly thumbed her way to the section on African gray parrots, and she reread the section she'd highlighted earlier.

The African gray parrot is one of the best-known mimics in the animal kingdom. These birds can imitate sounds from both animals and humans, as well as the world around them.

Abandoning the book, she revisited the sound of Mike engaging and disengaging the clinic's new dead bolt. The noise matched the beginning of Wilson's magnum opus, as Theresa called it. Could he be mimicking a lock engaging and disengaging?

Which meant the squeaking sound he made after the clicks could be a door with noisy hinges. Then came the sounds of someone saying "ow," a yipping noise, a deeper bark that could have passed for Murphy's, and then a thud.

She closed her eyes against the image of Murphy that bark had stirred in her at Theresa's house on Sunday morning—a sound Theresa had said Wilson was trying out for the first time that day.

Harriet opened her desk drawer and then pushed it closed. That could have been the thud Wilson made.

But the three clicks at the beginning and the end puzzled her. If someone clicked a lock three times, that meant they were either locking, unlocking, and then relocking—or unlocking, locking, and then unlocking again.

Shooting out of her chair, Harriet hurried into the clinic's reception area. "Mike? Polly? I need you to listen for a minute. Tell me what you hear." She took out her phone and played the recording she'd made of Wilson.

"I think I heard a couple of dogs in there, but I'm not sure about the other noises. Is this some kind of game you play in America?" Polly asked.

Harriet had to grin. "Not quite."

Mike wore a frown of concentration. "Can you play it again?"

"Yes. Ready?" At the handyman's nod, Harriet played the recording again. "Do you have a theory?"

"I might, but I don't want to say it," Mike said, looking down at his half-eaten treat.

Harriet grabbed his arm. "Please. I need help with these."

"There are two barking sounds, and they make me think of Princess and Murphy."

She stared at him. "*Princess?*"

"That sounded like her bark to me."

She stared at Mike as his words led to another possibility. "Maybe the 'ow' was the closest he could get to 'meow,'" she said.

"He who?" Polly cut in. "Harriet, what's going on?"

"I don't know yet. The sounds Mike made when he tested the new lock reminded me of some of the sounds Wilson has been making. The three clicks, the—"

And then she knew.

Three clicks for *three locks.*

There were three locks on the dilapidated shed she'd seen from Theresa's screened-in porch. If she had to guess, Harriet would say it was large enough to hold, say, a cat and two dogs. In a neighborhood where barking was commonplace.

Where a bird listened to everything with the help of a baby monitor.

Harriet ran into her office, snatched her keys off her desk, and dashed to the front door. "Polly, call Van and tell him to meet me at 4 Rocky Shore Drive. *Stat!*"

CHAPTER TWENTY-SEVEN

There was no sign of Van or any other police officers when she pulled up to the curb in front of Theo Littleton's house and shifted the Land Rover into park. Part of her knew the proper thing to do would be to wait for even one of them to arrive. But she couldn't.

She'd waited long enough—for Nessie, for Princess, for Murphy, for Grandad's painting.

For the truth.

She was confident she had the last one, and the sooner she confronted the man inside the house, the sooner she'd have the rest.

Harriet stepped out of the car and hurried up the front walk of the same cottage she'd stopped in front of mere days earlier. At the time, she'd been little more than thirty yards away from his first two captives, and she'd had no idea. How could she?

Yesterday and today, she'd been around the corner in Theresa's rental cottage, with Nessie, Princess, and Murphy roughly twenty-five yards away. And again, she hadn't known.

Wilson had been trying to tell them from the beginning. But she'd failed to truly hear him. It was a realization that both pained and angered her as she pounded her fist on the weather-beaten front door.

Seconds later, Harriet found herself staring into the eyes of a man she both disliked and pitied in equal parts. Disliked because of what he'd done to Nessie and Cindy, Harriet's boarders and their families, and her and Aunt Jinny. Pitied because he hadn't grown up at the hands of someone as positive and kind as Harold Bailey.

"What are you doing here?" Theo demanded.

"I'm here to help you make things right."

"Excuse me?"

"I think you know what I mean." She walked to the edge of the porch and gestured to the shed behind the house. "You're going to release the cat and two dogs you have locked in that shed for me now, or for the police when they arrive, which should be any minute. It's your choice."

Fear flashed across the man's narrow face, but it didn't last long. In fact, his expression quickly morphed to...*defiance*?

"I'll wait," he replied.

"Are you serious?" Harriet asked. "They're innocent animals."

"They served a purpose. Especially the two dogs."

"Their names are Princess and Murphy," she managed past gritted teeth. "What purpose did they serve?"

He smirked. "They've all but destroyed your precious business—the business your grandfather handed to you."

"And Nessie?" she asked. "Why take her?"

"She didn't exactly go as planned."

Her heart skipped a beat. "Did—did something happen to her? Did you hurt her?"

"No, she's fine," he sneered. "But her disappearance served to stir up all the old stories about Doc Bailey, the great savior. With no mention of my grandfather, despite how I spoon-fed his role to that reporter in one of my many emails and that lengthy conversation at the Crow's Nest. You'd think the person who spotted her between those rocks and made it so your grandfather could rescue her would matter. Without Felix Burton, there would've been no rescue. No Nessie. No big heartwarming gift to Cindy Summerton. And certainly no painting."

Relief made her sag against the exterior wall of the house. "And Grandad's painting?"

"Stealing that gave your family and you more press, more sympathy, more talk," Theo snapped. "It was infuriating."

"Did you leave the huge offer that made Candace Moore think I'd staged Nessie's abduction?"

His mouth moved upward in the first semblance of a smile she'd seen on his face. "I will say that was utter brilliance."

"So you stole Princess, knowing that would shake people's faith in me and the clinic."

"When I met Dale and witnessed the venom he had for you, I knew a stolen boarder on top of his one-star reviews would be enough to swing the pendulum away from you."

"In the hope it would swing toward you?" she suggested.

"Hardly. I knew that would never happen. I'm not a golden child born into a golden family. That's you. That's your father, I'm sure. That's your aunt, and your cousin. The whole Bailey family. I just wanted it to swing the adoration away from you. That was all I cared about."

A siren sounded in the distance. Harriet had to keep Theo talking. "Why? You don't even know me."

"I grew up hearing about Harold Bailey and his perfect life, the life he stole from my grandfather. When Grandpa died, I got *this* dump, *that* dump"—he pointed in the direction of Theresa's rental—"and the weed-infested scrap of land between them. When your grandfather died, you got an entire compound, complete with a house, a farm, a gallery, a barn, and a business, all in perfect condition."

There was that word again. Compound. A word he'd clearly used to reference Cobble Hill Farm in front of his tenant, his darts partner, and possibly Mike.

"You're so used to getting everything the easy way that you don't even see it," he hissed.

His words sank in.

"'I know you're used to everything going your way, but for once it's going mine,'" she quoted. "That's how you started the ransom note. You want me to have to pay for the things I want because you think I've been handed everything in my life. That my grandfather was handed everything in his life. That our whole family has had that."

"Because you have."

"You're wrong. My grandfather was respected and treasured by people in this community because of who he chose to be every morning he woke up—a God-fearing man who treated every human and animal he came across in a way that honored their Creator. My grandmother chose him because of that. His clinic thrived because of his approach. He left that clinic to me, but I show up every day and give it everything I've got every hour I'm there, making sure that every animal I see is cared for and every human they come with is treated with respect. I wasn't handed that by my grandfather. I chose to study it and to emulate it."

He made a production of yawning as the sirens drew nearer.

"How did you steal Murphy?" she asked. "How did you know the back door wasn't locked?"

"I didn't. I came prepared to pick it if you'd taken him into your house, as I suspected you would. I was more worried he would bark and alert you to my presence, but obviously he's used to meeting strangers."

Aware that Van and his fellow officer were parking on the street behind her, Harriet wrapped up her interrogation. "Last question. Gof, who wrote our last remaining negative review. I imagine that's you. It stands for 'Grandson of Felix' right?"

"Yes, and that review isn't going anywhere."

As Van and his coworker came up the steps, Harriet met and held Theo's angry gaze. "I feel sorry for Felix. And I feel sorry for you."

"Why?" Theo asked. "I did what he always wanted to. I crippled Cobble Hill Farm, not to mention the Bailey name."

"I feel sorry that that was something either of you wanted to begin with. It must feed into a sad, lonely life," Harriet told him.

"And you failed at it," Van pointed out as he snapped handcuffs around the other man's wrists. "The Baileys and Cobble Hill Farm are going to be respected around here for a long, long time."

Thirty minutes later, Harriet's clothes were covered in cat and dog hair as she beamed at the trio of reunions happening in front of her eyes. The excitement, the joy, the gratitude—emotions she too had felt when she'd opened the door of the shed to find Nessie's sleepy eyes, Princess's consternation, and Murphy's gloriously happy tail-wagging. Even the painting leaned against the back wall, slightly worse for wear after not being appropriately cared for in nearly a week with inclement weather.

It was a moment she knew she'd remember forever.

"I'm sorry about the damage he did to Doc Bailey's painting," Van said, stepping in beside Harriet. "Theo Littleton is clearly a bitter man. But he's a bitter man who'll be in jail with lots of time to think about the path he chose."

"The most important thing is that the animals are okay and back with their families," Harriet replied. "The painting has a little water damage and a little dirt, but I'm sure it can be repaired. I've already done some research about it on my phone, after I read Polly's text that clients have begun to reschedule with us."

Dale Renner had also called to let her know that Scout was feeling much better on the new diet, for which he'd thanked her profusely. She had to laugh when she heard Scout barking in the background, as if in agreement.

Van pulled a notebook and a pen from his shirt pocket. "How did you figure out the animals were here?"

Harriet chuckled. "I guess you could say a little bird told me."

At long last, Harriet walked through the front door of her beloved home at Cobble Hill Farm. She was pleasantly exhausted, and she couldn't have been happier with how the evening had turned out.

Until she rounded the corner into the living room and halted in her tracks.

There, sitting on her couch with broad smiles on their faces, sat her parents.

Harriet gasped. "What are you doing here?"

Mom rushed to her and wrapped her arms around Harriet. "We're here for Thanksgiving. We couldn't let you spend your first one in England without us. Jinny let us in. I hope that's okay."

"More than okay. I can't think of anything better."

As she sank into her parents' combined embrace, Harriet thought that perhaps this year, she had plenty to be thankful for after all.

FROM THE AUTHOR

Dear Reader,

When it came time to write this story, I knew that I wanted to include an African gray parrot as an important part of it. While I have never owned one, I've always been fascinated by their ability to mimic sounds. They listen to everything that happens around them, really hearing the sounds and words to be able to repeat them.

And for Harriet to get to the bottom of everything, she must also really listen and hear.

That's something I think we all need to do—with our family, our friends, and most importantly, with God.

I hope you enjoyed this story.

Signed,
Laura Bradford

ABOUT THE AUTHOR

While spending a rainy afternoon at a friend's house as a child, Laura Bradford fell in love with writing over a stack of blank paper, a box of crayons, and a freshly sharpened number-two pencil.

Today, Laura is the *USA Today* bestselling author of many cozy mystery series. She has also penned four Amish-based women's fiction novels set in and around Lancaster, PA. When she's not writing, Laura loves to bake, travel, and advocate for those living with MS.

TRUTH BEHIND THE FICTION

Wilson is an African gray parrot. African grays can live as long as eighty years, but forty to sixty is more the norm.

With such long lifespans, it is not unusual for these birds to outlive their owners.

They are also extremely sensitive animals. Changes in their environment can affect their behavior in many ways. Some signs of mental anguish in an African gray include feather plucking, a decrease in appetite, a disinterest in play, and less vocalizing.

Some research done on African grays compares their intelligence to that of a kindergarten student. They can mimic speech, be taught to answer questions, recognize colors, shapes, and letters, and even engage in some logical reasoning. While many of their words and phrases can be taught to them, they can also learn sounds on their own by simply paying attention—just as Wilson did.

YORKSHIRE YUMMIES

Banoffee Pie

Ingredients:

1½ cups graham cracker
    crumbs
⅓ cup sugar
6 tablespoons melted butter
1 (14-ounce) can dulce de leche

3 bananas, sliced
1½ cups heavy cream
3 tablespoons powdered sugar
Chocolate shavings

Directions:

Preheat oven to 350 degrees.

In medium bowl, mix together graham cracker crumbs, sugar, and melted butter.

Press into ungreased 9-inch pie pan.

Bake for 12 minutes or until set.

Cool baked crust on wire rack.

Spread dulce de leche in crust; arrange bananas evenly on top.

Beat heavy cream and powdered sugar in large bowl until stiff peaks form. Spread on top of pie filling.

Refrigerate pie for no less than 3 hours.

Sprinkle with chocolate shavings and serve!

The Christmas Camel Caper

BY JANE WILLAN

There was little Dr. Harriet Bailey loved more than a challenge. With her medical bag in one hand and a still-warm cranberry pie in the other, she hurried down the cobblestone street toward the White Church Christmas Fair. She was ready to assume her role as the on-duty vet for the live Nativity. The following day was the first Sunday of Advent, the usual weekend for White Church to host the annual event.

Although it wasn't the most direct route, she wound through the village on her way to the church so she could experience the enchanting atmosphere of White Church Bay at Christmas. Twinkling lights adorned each shop window. Festive music floated from overhead speakers, and the inviting aroma of hot chocolate wafted from the Happy Cup Tearoom and Bakery. She felt as if she had stepped right into a scene from Charles Dickens's *A Christmas Carol*.

The church steeple poked up from the far edge of the village with the bay sprawling beyond. She smiled, thinking about the

MYSTERIES OF COBBLE HILL FARM

upcoming live Nativity, which promised to be something special. Along with the customary sheep and donkeys, this year's animal selection showcased a new celebrity, a camel named Calvin.

She was glad for the long walk to the church. It gave her time to review her knowledge of camels, which she'd never treated before. They could drink salt water, their humps stored fat, and their nostrils sealed to prevent sand from flying up their noses. Despite their lumbering appearance, camels could zip along at up to forty miles per hour in short bursts. They also had a sweet tooth. Perhaps a sweet yet healthy Christmas snack would appeal to Calvin. Her dad would get a kick out of her brainstorming produce to share with a camel.

She had said goodbye to her parents the day before. They had flown in from Connecticut to spend Thanksgiving with her at Cobble Hill Farm, the property she'd inherited from her late grandfather. It had been a wonderful time together, but now, all the holiday lights and Christmas cheer made her wish they'd been able to stay.

She paused at the window of Tales & Treasures, a corner shop that sold books and even toys, to collect herself. Amid holiday cookbooks and Advent calendars, a children's book lay open, its pages displaying a radiant star. The inscription beneath read: THE STAR THEY HAD SEEN IN THE EAST GUIDED THEM TO THE PLACE WHERE THE CHILD WAS.

As she admired the artist's depiction of the brilliant star against the night sky, she experienced a moment of clarity. God's light could guide her, as it had guided the magi. Resolved to find the spirit and joy of Christmas in White Church Bay despite her parents' absence, she took a deep breath and continued down the street. Time to concentrate on her work.

The live Nativity hummed with activity. Church members, clad in makeshift biblical attire of bathrobes, sandals, and thick socks, were stationed around the stable. A miniature donkey shared the scene with three goats, two sheep, and a beautiful Belgian hare. The baby Jesus gurgled with happiness from the manger under the watchful eyes of Mary and Joseph.

Calvin the camel stood apart, his tall, elegant frame towering over the Bethlehem tableau. Harriet immediately loved his velvety muzzle and large, expressive eyes. He seemed to observe everything with a mixture of curiosity and apprehension. "Hello, you beautiful boy," she greeted him, patting his shaggy neck in an attempt to soothe any nerves he might feel.

Ethan Grimshaw, a skilled farrier she'd met since moving to Yorkshire, approached her with his lanky gait. His tall frame and broad shoulders were complemented by a warm smile that lit his ruggedly handsome face. His sandy-brown hair was worn longer than most men in the village chose to go, giving him a tousled yet charming appearance.

Ethan ran a mobile business from his van, equipped with every tool needed for his trade, offering his services across the region. Though new to the area, he was establishing Yorkshire as his home and business hub. He had reached out to Harriet for client leads, and he was integrating himself into the community's daily life.

Harriet had checked his references and then recommended him to a horse owner nearby. Ethan had soon shown that he was talented and hardworking, and he had already proved a useful connection for Harriet as well. Just last week, he'd crafted special shoes for a Shetland pony with a unique condition that made it hard to walk, and a few days later, its young owner had sent Harriet a video of the pony trotting joyfully around the barnyard.

"How's the big guy doing?" Ethan asked Harriet with a nod to Calvin. Ethan's cheerful voice matched his welcoming smile and warm brown eyes. He immediately came off as approachable, someone to chat with over a cup of coffee or rely on in a pinch. She could see why her clients liked him.

Harriet reached up to scratch behind Calvin's ear. "He's fine, Ethan." She placed a stethoscope against the camel's chest and listened. "His heart rate's a little fast, but nothing to worry about." She coiled the stethoscope and slid it into her bag. "As an equine specialist, are you as intrigued by camels as I am?"

"Not really." Ethan shrugged. "Camels and horses have very little in common, despite being used for the same kinds of tasks in different parts of the world. Besides, since they don't wear shoes, I never work with them."

"Of course," she said. "But they have a similar nobility, don't you think?"

He grinned at her. "Is there any animal in which you don't find a certain nobility?"

"Probably not. I even adore Dottie, Lloyd Throckmorton's armadillo who's been coming to Cobble Hill for a long time."

He laughed. "That's what makes you such a good vet. You can find beauty in even an elderly armadillo." He glanced at his cell phone. "I'm off for an appointment with Lord Miltshire. His chestnut mare threw a shoe, and he wants me to tend to her straightaway."

"Take a piece of my cranberry pie. You'll need something for the drive."

"Thanks for the offer, but I don't have time. Best of luck with the manger menagerie, though."

She watched him navigate through the Nativity crowd, heading for his brightly painted van parked by the parish graveyard entrance. Emblazoned on the side was Ethan's logo, a stylized anvil and horse-shoe alongside the name of his business, GALLOP & FORGE FARRIERY SERVICES in bold letters.

Calvin stamped his front feet, as if demanding Harriet's attention.

"Calm down, my friend," she told him. "It's going to be a long day. Save your energy."

She checked his water and hay then stood with him until he relaxed, the camel's eyes with their long, curled lashes almost closing in the morning sun.

Harriet checked on the other animals then meandered through the churchyard, chatting with an angel who had paired a set of glittery wings with sneakers, and the actor playing Joseph, who had left the stable to stretch his legs and enjoy a cup of tea.

In the everyday world, "Joseph" was better known as Mark Butler, a local dentist who also directed the White Church youth group. "What do you think of our Bethlehem star?" He pointed to the roof of the manger. The star, a concoction of glitter and sturdy pasteboard, appeared pieced together with an abundance of glue. "Eloise Pennington helped the kids make it," Mark said. "You've met her, haven't you? She's one of White Church Bay's resident artists. She seemed to have a lot of fun making the star and the other decorations with the kids."

"It's very artistic," Harriet replied with a smile. "I've never seen pasteboard quite so resplendent."

The sight of the star with all its glue and glitter reminded her of her grandad's tales of a very different star—one made of pure silver and encrusted with sapphires. At the beginning of the twentieth century, an anonymous benefactor had gifted it to the village. It was meant to be a symbol of God's light shining through the darkness. Since 1919, villagers had gathered for the midnight Christmas Eve service at White Church, where they'd watch the star be placed atop the church tree. This year, she would finally witness the tradition herself.

A bellow reverberated through the quiet air, and the tranquil scene exploded. Calvin plunged through the gate of his pen, charged across the churchyard, and paused for a moment in the middle of the road past the church. Nativity participants scattered, a car screeched to a sudden stop, and pedestrians froze, staring. Calvin sniffed the air then swung around and galloped off toward the village center, his padded feet thudding on the cobblestones.

Shouts erupted from the crowd as Calvin raced out of sight, easily outpacing anyone who chased him. He even bumped into a caroler as he passed, sending the man's sheet music flying.

Harriet dashed after him, with Pastor Fitzwilliam "Will" Knight on her heels. When they finally caught up with the runaway camel, Calvin stood in Miss Jane Birtwhistle's winter cabbages, his head buried in a large wicker basket among the frosty cruciferous leaves. He lifted his majestic head to gaze at them as if wondering what all the fuss was about.

She caught a whiff of sweetness in the air, and her eyes landed on the sticky substance at the basket's bottom, the same stuff that coated Calvin's lips. "Figs," she said, grabbing Calvin's halter. "He picked up their scent all the way from the church."

"That's quite the nose you've got there," Will said to Calvin. "It must be your superpower." The pastor of White Church was always quick to smile, an honest smile that said he was genuinely glad to see his parishioners. He was easily one of the kindest people Harriet had ever met, a man who walked the walk of his faith and went far beyond simply preaching it from the pulpit.

"Camels have a keen sense of smell and can sniff out food from great distances. It's an ability that helps them survive in the desert." She led Calvin out of the cabbages. "It's natural that he likes figs, as camels often enjoy sweets."

"Not just figs," Will said. He picked up the basket and peered inside. "Figgy pudding."

"How do you know?"

"Because I know a good figgy pudding when I meet one, even if it's been half devoured by a greedy camel. And I believe your aunt Jinny's award-winning figgy pudding went missing this morning from the Christmas fair."

Harriet's aunt, Dr. Jinny Garrett, lived in the dower cottage at Cobble Hill Farm. Getting to be so close to her was one of Harriet's favorite things about her move to Yorkshire.

"How would Aunt Jinny's figgy pudding end up in a basket in Jane Birtwhistle's cabbages?"

Will shrugged. "Stranger things have happened at the Christmas fair."

"Like what?" They fell into step as they headed back to the live Nativity, Calvin in tow.

"Well, there was the great glitter bomb incident a few years ago, and who could forget the eggnog fountain fiasco the year before that?"

She laughed. "So what will future generations call today's excitement?"

"How about 'The Christmas Camel Caper'?"

As she laughed with him, it hit her again how much she really liked Will. He was funny, genuinely kind, and so easy to talk to. Sharing a laugh with him felt like the most natural thing in the world. And she had to admit he was attractive. Feeling her cheeks warm, she focused on adjusting Calvin's halter to hide her blush. She didn't know what Will felt about her—if anything. And she wasn't ready to show her feelings yet, especially since they were so new.

When they returned to the church with the wayward camel in tow, Will headed off to check in with other participants of the fair. She guided Calvin back into his pen, reflecting that he was probably ready for a long nap after his adventure and snack.

Once she had him settled, she checked the gate. The latch hadn't been broken. Calvin must have bumped it just right with his substantial nose. She secured the latch then wrapped it with several layers of medical tape from her bag to prevent Calvin from escaping again. She left him dozing then checked the other animals again.

A sharp cry of alarm sliced the air. Will stood rooted to the spot on the front steps of the church. "It's gone!" he shouted. "The silver Christmas star is gone!"

A NOTE FROM THE EDITORS

We hope you enjoyed another exciting volume in the Mysteries of Cobble Hill Farm series, published by Guideposts. For over seventy-five years, Guideposts, a nonprofit organization, has been driven by a vision of a world filled with hope. We aspire to be the voice of a trusted friend, a friend who makes you feel more hopeful and connected.

By making a purchase from Guideposts, you join our community in touching millions of lives, inspiring them to believe that all things are possible through faith, hope, and prayer. Your continued support allows us to provide uplifting resources to those in need. Whether through our communities, websites, apps, or publications, we inspire our audiences, bring them together, and comfort, uplift, entertain, and guide them. Visit us at guideposts.org to learn more.

We would love to hear from you. Write us at Guideposts, P.O. Box 5815, Harlan, Iowa 51593 or call us at (800) 932-2145. Did you love *A Little Bird Told Me*? Leave a review for this product on guideposts.org/shop. Your feedback helps others in our community find relevant products.

Find inspiration, find faith, find Guideposts.
Shop our best sellers and favorites at
guideposts.org/shop
Or scan the QR code to go directly to our Shop

Find more inspiring stories in these best-loved Guideposts fiction series!

Mysteries of Lancaster County

Follow the Classen sisters as they unravel clues and uncover hidden secrets in Mysteries of Lancaster County. As you get to know these women and their friends, you'll see how God brings each of them together for a fresh start in life.

Secrets of Wayfarers Inn

Retired schoolteachers find themselves owners of an old warehouse-turned-inn that is filled with hidden passages, buried secrets, and stunning surprises that will set them on a course to puzzling mysteries from the Underground Railroad.

Tearoom Mysteries Series

Mix one stately Victorian home, a charming lakeside town in Maine, and two adventurous cousins with a passion for tea and hospitality. Add a large scoop of intriguing mystery, and sprinkle generously with faith, family, and friends, and you have the recipe for *Tearoom Mysteries*.

Ordinary Women of the Bible

Richly imagined stories—based on facts from the Bible—have all the plot twists and suspense of a great mystery, while bringing you fascinating insights on what it was like to be a woman living in the ancient world.

To learn more about these books, visit Guideposts.org/Shop